"You're never going to get over him, are you?"

Stephanie's eyes widened as Gray continued.

"You're never going to let him go. You carry him about in your head with you. He shares your bed at night—" He broke off abruptly and said in a different voice, "When you touched me this afternoon, were you pretending then that I was him?"

"No—no, of course I wasn't!" Stephanie cried in stunned surprise. "I did that to protect you, to—to...if Carla's husband had seen the two of you together. I—"

"You were only thinking of me, is that it? Well, perhaps it's time I repaid the favor, and reminded you exactly what it is you're turning your back on by clinging to your memories of a dead man."

Stephanie panicked. Nothing made sense anymore—especially Gray's mouth descending on hers!

PENNY JORDAN was constantly in trouble in school because of her inability to stop daydreaming—especially during French lessons. In her teens she was an avid romance reader, although it didn't occur to her to try writing one herself until she was older. "My first half-dozen attempts ended up ingloriously," she remembers, "but I persevered, and one manuscript was finished." She plucked up the courage to send it to a publisher, convinced her book would be rejected. It wasn't and the rest is history! Penny is married and lives in Cheshire.

Books by Penny Jordan

Don't miss any of our special offers. Write to us at the following address for information on our newest releases.

Harlequin Reader Service
901 Fuhrmann Blvd., P.O. Box 1397, Buffalo, NY 14240
Canadian address: P.O. Box 603,
Fort Erie, Ont. L2A 5X3

PENNY JORDAN

substitute lover

Harlequin Books

TORONTO • NEW YORK • LONDON
AMSTERDAM • PARIS • SYDNEY • HAMBURG
STOCKHOLM • ATHENS • TOKYO • MILAN

Harlequin Presents first edition September 1988
ISBN 0-373-11105-3

Original hardcover edition published in 1987
by Mills & Boon Limited

CHAPTER ONE

AHEAD of her loomed the motorway exit sign for the village. Stephanie sighed faintly, the soft sound whispering past vulnerably curved lips. The late afternoon sunlight burnished her long hair into a shining copper cloak. Normally she wore it up in a neat chignon, but today she had left it loose.

Only the inward clenching of her stomach muscles betrayed her growing tension. She hated coming back so much. Fear and pain mingled inside her, making her fingers grip harder on the steering-wheel.

If it wasn't for Gray ... She shuddered visibly, aching to close her eyes and blot out the terrible images blocking out the gentle, rolling countryside and the wide span of the motorway.

Never, ever, no matter how long she lived, would she forget that terrible night when they had come to tell her that Paul was dead. The shock of it, coming so quickly on the heels of that last bitter quarrel, had produced a burden of guilt she carried with her still.

Even now, ten years later, she often woke in the night re-living that last fatal evening they had spent together. The quarrel had blown up over nothing—and it had not been the first time. After only three months of marriage Paul had become a stranger—a frighteningly violent stranger, too, at times—who called her frigid and sexless, and complained that he wished he had never married her.

He had stormed out of the cottage and she had let him, too confused and miserable to try and coax him back.

It had been a bad summer, with constant gales and dangerous seas. She had never dreamed that he intended to take out his boat, but he had. Who knew what thoughts had been in his mind in those last few hours of his life? The seas had been far too dangerous for a lone yachtsman, so the coastguard had told them, and Paul, reckless as always, had omitted to wear his buoyancy jacket and safety harness.

He had been swept overboard by one of the giant waves, or so the authorities surmised, because his body had been found on a beach by an early morning stroller.

His grief-stricken parents had demanded to know why she hadn't alerted the coastguard earlier, when he had not come home, and Stephanie had been forced to lie, unwilling to add to their pain by telling them that there had been other nights during their brief marriage when he hadn't come home, when she had slept alone in the wide double bed she had grown to hate. But John and Elise Chalmers had worshipped their only child, and she had not had the heart to destroy their image of him.

She knew that they blamed her for his death, and in her heart of hearts she felt equally guilty. If she had been a different type of woman ... if she had had the sexuality to keep Paul at her side, he would not have grown bored with her company ... would not have been driven by the relentless devil that possessed him, unleashing a streak of violence in him that she had never suspected existed.

They had married too young and on too short an acquaintance; she knew that now. Neither of them had really known the other, and by the time they realised how intrinsically different they were it was too late— they were married.

Tears stung her eyes briefly, her guilt momentarily overlaid by sorrow. Paul had been so alive . . . so good-looking and arrogantly male. She had stopped loving him within weeks of their marriage—the first time he had hit her he had destroyed her image of him and with it her almost childish adoration; but that did not stop her regretting his death and the waste of such a very young life.

Only Gray had stood up for her and said in that quiet, slow voice of his that she was not to blame for Paul's death. But Gray didn't know the truth. Even now he still didn't know the truth, but his defence of her, the way his arms had held her, comforting and protecting her in the shocking aftermath of the news, had formed a bond between them that nothing could ever break.

Automatically she turned off the motorway, taking the pretty country road that dipped between the gentle hills and then meandered through the New Forest down to the coast. Her bright yellow VW preferred the gentle pace of country driving, the engine almost purring as the motorway was completely lost from sight and they were swallowed up by golden fields, ripely heavy with their summer crop.

Her friends in London teased her about her devotion

to her little car. She earned a good living from her work as an illustration artist, and then additionally there was the income she derived from her share in the boat-yard that had been in Paul's family for several generations.

She always felt uncomfortable about that inheritance, but Gray had urged her not to dispose of it, and she had agreed. Now that Paul's parents were dead, she and Gray were joint owners of the yard.

Pauls and Gray's grandfather had started it, passing it on to his two sons.

Gray's parents had been killed in a sailing accident when he was fourteen years old, and he had virtually been brought up alongside his cousin. But Paul had never really liked Gray. She had known that from the first and had put the animosity between them down to the seven-year age-gap. As a teenager, newly arrived in the area, she had found Gray both distant and rather formidable.

It had been her father's interest in boats that had led to her introduction to Paul. The boat-yard was one of his accounts at the branch of the bank he had just been transferred to as manager, and he had taken Stephanie with him, on a visit to inspect the yard.

Paul had been working in the yard, a slim, golden-haired young god with a deep tan and a self-assured smile.

She had thought their love was mutual, but she realised now that to Paul she had only been a new challenge. He had a reputation locally as something of a playboy, but she hadn't known that then.

She had been a rather shy teenager, a product of an

all-girls' school, studious and not as knowledgeable about sex as most of her peers.

She had just left school, and had been looking forward to going to art school after the long summer break. And then she had met Paul.

Within days they were virtually inseparable. When Paul discovered her reservations about allowing him to make love to her, and the fact that she was still a virgin, he had announced that they would get married.

That had been typical of his impulsiveness and his determination to have his own way, Stephanie had recognised later, but at the time she had been too bemused to do anything but follow where he led. Of course they had encountered massive parental objections, from both families; but the more their parents urged them to wait, the more determined Paul became that they would not.

Even Gray had suggested that they get to know one another a little better before making such an important commitment, but Paul had laughed at him, she remembered, sneering that since Gray was not married himself he was not qualified to speak.

In the end their parents had given way, perhaps in the fear that if they did not, they might do something even more reckless . . . and who knew . . . perhaps they would have done. Paul had whispered on more than one occasion that if it was the only way, they could start a baby. 'Then they'll have to let us get married,' he had coaxed.

Whether or not she would have gone that far she didn't know. Certainly she had been bemused enough by her feelings for him to do almost anything he suggested. Her parents had tried to tell her that she was suffering from a classic case of infatuation but she hadn't wanted to know ... she hadn't wanted to believe them.

In the end, Paul had got his way. They had had a small family wedding, she had worn a white dress; and they had moved into a pretty cottage down near the harbour that Paul's parents had bought for them. Mr and Mrs Chalmers had a large house just outside the village, and Gray lived in what had been his grandfather's cottage quite close to the boat-yard.

Their honeymoon had been a bitter disappointment—for both of them. Paul did not have the patience or the experience to arouse her to the point where she could enjoy his lovemaking, and he had swiftly grown impatient and then angry with her for her lack of response.

The first time he had hit her had been after a quarrel, and she had been too shocked to do anything other than stare at him. Her father had never raised a hand to her in all her life, and the cruelty of Paul's blow hurt her emotions more than her flesh.

Of course, he had immediately been contrite; they had made up their quarrel and he had sworn never to touch her in anger again.

Within days he had broken that promise and, by the time their honeymoon was over, Stephanie had learned to fear her new husband's sudden surges of temper.

She returned to her new home and her new life sick at heart and cowed in spirit.

People noticed of course, especially her parents, but

she had too much pride to tell them the truth. Inwardly she felt, as Paul claimed, that she was to blame for his violence, that she invited it in some way, and deserved it for her inability to respond to him as a woman.

His violence towards her quickly escalated to the point where she cringed every time he came near her.

They stopped making love within days of returning to their new home, and quite soon after that Paul started staying out later and later at night, and then not coming home at all.

He had made no secret of the fact that there were other girls, but whenever she suggested that they end the marriage he had flown into one of his almost maniacal tempers, and she soon learned not to bring the subject up.

His death might have freed her from the physical violence of their marriage, but emotionally she was still trapped, both in her own guilt for failing him as a woman, and her fear that she was somehow not like other members of her sex—not capable of responding sexually to anyone's embrace.

Her memories of the unhappiness of the few short months of her marriage, and the guilt feelings that had come afterwards, were so strong, that she hated returning to the village.

Paul's parents no longer lived there—they had moved away shortly after his death, when Paul's father had sold out his share of the boat-yard to Gray. Now they were both dead, increasing her sense of guilt. They had both adored Paul, worshipped him almost, seeing no fault in him.

Stephanie's own pride had made it impossible for

her to discuss with anyone the cruelty of Paul's
treatment of her, and so it remained locked inside her,
a dark, unhappy secret that still had the power to
destroy her sleep.

There had been no man in her life since Paul. What
would have been the point? She would only have
incited them to violence once they discovered her lack
of sexuality. Gray was the only man in her life, and
their relationship was a sexless, friendly one that could
quite easily have existed between two members of the
same sex.

The road crested a hill. To her left she could see the
bright glitter of the river, slow and majestic in its
steady progress towards the sea.

Soon she would be there. A quiver of apprehension
ran through her, all her doubts and dreads about the
wisdom of obeying Gray's request that she come down
here betrayed in the cloudy darkness of her eyes.

Her body—too slim and fragile, perhaps, for a
woman of twenty-eight—tensed, ready to absorb the
shock of pain and guilt that waited for her with her
first glimpse of the estuary and the sea.

It was a small place, the village, where everyone
knew everyone else. They all knew about her loss;
about Paul's death, but none of them knew about her
deeper anguish. Perhaps fearing his parents' discover-
ing the truth, Paul had gone into Southampton on
those nights when he didn't return home, and had
found there, or so he had told her, the sexual
satisfaction he could not get from her, his wife.

Cold . . . frigid. The accusations, so well remembered, hammered against her skull, turning her skin pale with anguish.

If only Gray had come up to London to discuss the business of the boat-yard with her, as he had done in the past, but this time he had been insistent that she return here. He had even threatened to come and get her if she refused and, knowing he meant it, she had eventually, reluctantly, given way.

Perhaps in her shoes another woman might have tried to prove Paul's accusations wrong by taking one lover after another, but Stephanie couldn't do that. She was too afraid that Paul had been right. She had failed with him, and she would fail with anyone else.

Instead, she had locked herself away behind the barrier of her guilt, using Paul as an excuse for not forming any new relationships. No other man was going to get an opportunity to abuse her physically, or hurt and betray her because she couldn't satisfy him; no other man was going to turn from her to someone else, as Paul had done.

Not even Gray had known, as she wept in his arms, that she cried not just for Paul himself but for the betrayal of their love and her own failure to prove herself a woman. And he would never know it.

The village was in sight now, and she automatically tensed her muscles, glancing at her watch. Gone six o'clock, but Gray would probably still be at the boat-yard. She would go there first, rather than the cottage.

Gray lived there alone now and had done for several years. The shock of losing her son had led to Paul's mother's death, and Paul's father, Gray's uncle, had died two years later from a heart attack. Now only Gray was left.

The boat-yard was on the far side of the village, right down on the bank of the estuary. It had been in Gray's family for about a hundred years.

As she parked her VW and climbed out of it, Gray emerged from his office and came towards her. Tall, with forbiddingly broad shoulders and a shock of night-black hair, he was a commandingly masculine man. Densely blue eyes studied her and, shockingly, Stephanie momentarily recognised in them the age-old appraisal of a man looking at a woman.

Gray moved and the appraisal was gone, leaving her to suspect that she must have imagined it.

The late afternoon breeze coming off the estuary flattened the silky curve of her skirt against her hip and the long line of her legs. She lifted a hand to push her hair back off her face and heard Gray growl, 'You're getting too thin. What have you been doing to yourself?'

'I'm not thin, just fashionably slim!' she protested.

He was wearing an old pair of jeans that clung to his body like a second skin. Hastily averting her eyes from the powerful muscles of his thighs, she was tensely aware of his eyes narrowing.

'What's wrong? You're as skittish as a dinghy without a tiller.'

His fingers closed over her arm, drawing her towards him. She could smell the familiar male scent of his body, and felt an almost uncontrollable urge to cling to him and let him stand between her and her pain.

'You know coming down here always affects me like this.'

Instead of comforting her as he normally did, he released her almost abruptly.

'After ten years?' There was something almost sardonic about the way he said it. 'That's one hell of a long time to grieve, Steph.'

Before she could comment, the office door opened and a stunning blonde came out. Dressed in tight white jeans and a brief silky top, she swayed provocatively towards them.

'I've still got a few things to do down here.' Gray glanced towards the blonde. 'I'll take you up to the cottage and join you there later.'

Stephanie always stayed at the cottage when she visited Gray. The village had no hotel, and besides, where else should she stay? But now some contrariness made her glance across at the blonde walking towards them, her mouth curling slightly as she asked, 'Are you sure you want me to stay with you, Gray? I don't want to be in the way.'

She saw his mouth tighten. 'Well now, that's quite a question. What made you ask it, I wonder?'

For some reason she had annoyed him. Conscious of the blonde watching them, Stephanie took a deep breath.

'Nothing at all. I just wondered if your girlfriend might object?'

'Girlfriend?' His dark head swivelled to look at the blonde. She smiled back, teasingly. She was older than Stephanie had first imagined, and she was wearing a wedding ring, but that meant nothing these days.

'Carla won't mind. She knows that we're old friends.'

As though to prove the point he called over casually to the blonde, 'I'm just taking Stephanie back to the cottage. I won't be long.'

Stephanie had to run to keep up with his long-legged stride as he walked towards her VW. Watching him fold himself inside reminded her of how tall and broad he was, the play of hard muscles beneath his skin alienly male.

She just wasn't used to being this close to a man . . . any man, she told herself as she drove the car towards the cottage; that was why she was so conscious of Gray's masculinity.

'I've put you in the far bedroom,' he told her laconically as he opened the cottage door. 'I'll leave you to get yourself settled in. I'll be back in half an hour. I've just got one or two things to finish off.'

'Half an hour. I'm sure Carla would be very flattered if she heard that.'

Suddenly conscious of how waspish and acid she sounded, Stephanie turned away from him. What was the matter with her? Gray had had girlfriends before. He was one of the most eligible men on the estuary. Physically, he was everything a woman could want in a man; he was also kind and gentle. Strange that at thirty-four-odd he should still be unmarried, and stranger still that she had never questioned his lack of a wife before.

'Oh, I'm sure I could think of a way to make amends.' He said it so softly that the words shivered across her skin, the look in his eyes as she turned to stare at him making her own widen with shocked pain.

Gray was her friend. He knew how much she loathed anything that had the slightest sexual connotation, and yet here he was deliberately making her aware of his sexuality, of the very masculine side of him that he had previously held in check.

Before she could protest he said bleakly, 'Don't provoke me, Steph, I'm not in the mood for it.'

As he turned away from her she recognised that she was not the only one who had lost weight; he too was slightly thinner, his profile carved in slightly harder lines. Was something wrong? Was that why he wanted to see her? Was that why he was acting so oddly? From the time of Paul's death he had been her friend, he had supported and protected her, and she had come to lean on him, to trust him, as she knew she could never trust anyone else, but now . . .

He paused at the door and turned towards her.

'Not everyone's like you, Steph,' he told her harshly. 'We haven't all abdicated from the human race, and the needs and emotions that go with being human.'

Stephanie recoiled as though he had hit her. In all the years they had been friends, Gray had never once spoken to her like that. Never once looked at her the way he was looking at her right now, with his mouth twisted and his eyes hard and accusing.

'Gray . . .' Panic filled her voice and her eyes. What was happening to them? She was losing him . . . losing his friendship . . . she could sense it, feel it almost . . .

'I'll see you later.'

He was gone before she could object. Numbly she stared at the closed door. What was happening? A tiny frisson of fear trembled through her. She wandered uneasily round the small sitting-room. The cottage was very old, the rooms low-ceilinged and beamed. She sat down in one of the chintz-covered chairs and stared unseeingly into the empty fireplace. The horse brasses, collected by Gray's mother, shone against the buttermilk-coloured walls, the soft salt-laden breeze flowing in through one of the open lattice windows. The room was as familiar to Stephanie as her London flat, although she could count on the fingers of one hand the number of times she had been here since Paul's death. The house had been let while Gray lived with Paul's parents, but as soon as he was eighteen he had announced that he was moving into his parents' old home. There had never been the rapport between Gray and Paul's parents that had existed between them and their own child. Many, many times he must have felt shut out, but to his credit he had never let it show ... never resented Paul in the way that the younger man had resented him. They had never discussed Paul's animosity towards him; the past was a closed book and one which she had assumed neither of them wished to open.

She had never thought of Gray in any male or sexual sense, but today, shockingly, she had looked at him and seen not her friend, but a man with sexual desires and drives like any other.

A curious, aching pain built up inside her and spread tormentingly through her body. What was wrong with her? Was she really so insecure that she feared the thought of sharing Gray with someone else? She had always known that he didn't live the life of a

monk ... but until today she had never come face to
face with the reality of his sexuality, and she was
shocked by her own reaction to it. Instead of feeling
nothing, she had felt a surprising degree of jealousy.
But why?

And why had Gray been so offhand, almost angry
with her? Normally he greeted her with a warm hug
and a welcoming smile, but not this time—not today.
Had it been because Carla had been there? It shocked
her how much she had missed that brief, warm contact
with his body. Confused by the chaos of her thoughts
and feelings, she tried to dismiss them as a natural
result of her return to the place where she had known
such pain and misery, but something deep inside her
refused to be convinced.

Angry with herself, Stephanie went outside to her
car and brought in her suitcase. She didn't intend
staying for more than a couple of days, and it didn't
take her long to unpack her things and put them away.
The room she was sleeping in had sloping eaves and a
tiny window that overlooked the wild tangle of the
cottage garden, and the hills beyond. The cottage had
four bedrooms, and this one had once been Gray's.

Now he slept in the large double bedroom which had
once been his parents', and as she stepped out on to the
landing something made her hesitate and then slowly
push open the door to Gray's room.

He had an experienced sailor's neatness. Nothing
was out of place. An old-fashioned four-poster bed
dominated the room, and against her will Stephanie's
eyes were drawn to it. How many women had shared it
with Gray over the years? None of them would have

been like her, frigid and undesirable. A lump gathered painfully in her chest, a familiar sense of anguish enveloping her. She didn't want to be the way she was. She . . .

'Looking for something?'

The unexpectedly harsh sound of Gray's voice behind her made her jump. She turned round sharply, stumbling in shock. She hadn't heard him come in.

Instantly his arms came out to steady her. Although it had been months since he last held her, she was immediately aware of a sense of homecoming and security. Without being aware of what she was doing, she snuggled up against him, sighing faintly.

'For God's sake, Stephanie!'

Instantly she stiffened in his arms, suddenly conscious of the hard thud of his heart and the heat coming off his body.

'What the hell are you doing? Dreaming about Paul? He's dead, Stephanie. Dead. And for all the living you do, you might as well be, too. Hasn't there been anyone in these last ten years?'

'I don't want that sort of relationship in my life. You know that.' She had to turn her head so that he couldn't look at her.

As his arms dropped away from her, he said flatly, 'We . . . you can't go on living like this, Steph. It's not . . .'

'Not what? Not "natural"? Is that what you're going to say, Gray? That *I'm* not "natural"?'

Her overwrought nerves shrieked in protest as she flung the words at him.

He seemed to be looking at her with an odd mixture

of pain and defeat in his eyes. Her breath locked in her throat, tears not far away. What on earth was happening to them? She and Gray had been so close, such good friends, and now . . . and now they seemed to be teetering on the brink of destroying all that they had shared.

He made a slight movement, a reaching out towards her from which she immediately recoiled, her expression proud and tortured as she cried out painfully, 'You want the truth, Gray? All right, I'll give it to you. I don't have the least interest in sex.' She took a deep, rather shaky breath. 'I'm frigid, Gray.' There, she'd said it; she'd admitted at last the agonising lack of sexuality that had caused her so much pain.

'Steph!'

She heard the shock in Gray's voice, but she couldn't respond to it; couldn't listen to any more questions now, however well meant. Gray cared for her as a friend, and would want to help her, but this was one problem that no one else could help with.

Suddenly she had an overwhelming need to be alone.

'I . . . I think I'd better find somewhere else to stay tonight, Gray, I . . .'

She saw from the look on his face that she had hurt and angered him. So many gulfs were springing up between them, so many barriers that couldn't be crossed.

She made a dash for her room and privacy, coming to an abrupt halt as Gray's fingers tightened round her wrist, holding her prisoner. Shock had darkened his eyes to dense sapphire, his mouth a hard line of disbelief as he shook her.

'What the hell is this, Steph? Is that really what you think? That you're frigid?'

'Isn't it what *you* think?' As she stood there, trembling, Stephanie wondered frantically what on earth had happened between them to promote this conversation. Talking about her relationship with Paul and the flaws in her femininity wasn't something she had ever wanted to do, least of all with Gray, who, friend though he was, was also so undeniably male that he made her acutely aware of the pathetic shortcomings in her own personality. Instinctively, without knowing how she possessed that knowledge, she knew that as a lover Gray would be both skilled and tender.

Dragging her mind away from such provocative thoughts she saw that he was frowning.

'I don't make those kind of assumptions without some hard facts to back them up. As I haven't been to bed with you, I don't know, do I?'

It was what he hadn't said rather than what he had that shocked her speechless.

'I'll wash and then we'll have something to eat. I've got a lot to talk over with you.'

His calm words broke the spell that had held her silent.

'Won't Carla object to your spending the evening with me?'

His eyebrows lifted. 'Why should she? She knows that we're old friends.'

To her chagrin, Stephanie realised that he was looking amused.

'Why don't you go down and make us some coffee?

And then over dinner I'll show you the plans of the new boat I'm working on.'

This was the Gray she knew ... her friend. The tension that had engulfed her earlier eased. Feeling relieved, she hurried downstairs to the kitchen.

Mrs Ames, Gray's daily, had left a casserole ready-prepared in the fridge, and one of her famous apple pies.

Although the cottage had a pretty dining-room, normally when she came to stay they ate off trays in the sitting-room. It was more cosy.

It didn't take long to make the coffee and, wanting to make amends for her earlier childishness, Stephanie poured some into a mug for Gray and took it upstairs.

His bedroom door was open. She could smell the clean, pine-fresh scent of his soap, and from behind the closed door of his bathroom she could hear him singing.

Her mouth curved into a brief grin as she recognised the familiar sound of an old sea shanty. It was one Gray only sang when he was feeling particularly happy. Perhaps she had been wrong about there being some serious problem with the boat-yard.

Knocking briefly on his open door, she walked into his bedroom. She had been silly to get so upset simply because he had asked about her as a friend. Not knowing the truth, he had simply thought that she had grieved for Paul for long enough.

But now that he did know the truth ... he had not exhibited the shock she might have expected. Lost in thought, she gnawed worriedly at her lower lip.

The door to Gray's bathroom opened and he walked into the bedroom, plainly unaware that she was there.

His hair was damp and he was towelling it roughly. The rest of his body . . . Scarlet faced, Stephanie stood rooted to the spot, totally unable to move, as she slowly absorbed the details of his nude body.

Gray only realised that she was there when he threw down the towel. Transfixed with shock and embarrassment, Stephanie gulped as he walked past her and gently closed the bedroom door.

'I . . . I brought you a cup of coffee.'

Her voice was a thick, unfamiliar croak, but at least speaking freed her from her momentary paralysis. She turned to flee and discovered that somehow Gray was standing in front of the door.

'Thank you.' He said it gently, casually reaching out to take the mug from her. Hideously embarrassed, Stephanie looked everywhere but at him. Why, oh why had she walked into his bedroom in the first place? She had *known* that he was having a shower.

'What's the matter, Steph?' His voice was as soft as silk, but still she couldn't look at him. 'You've seen me working on the boats wearing not that much more.'

'That . . . that was different.' She was having difficulty in swallowing.

'Not that much surely. I'm the one who should be embarrassed, you know.'

Maybe he *should* be, but he certainly wasn't. Why on earth didn't he put some clothes on?

As though he read her mind, he moved to one side, opening a drawer and casually pulling out socks and underpants.

'Pass me that shirt on the bed, will you?'

He sounded so casually at ease that Stephanie found

she was doing what he asked almost without thinking. By the time she had handed it to him, he was already wearing the brief dark-coloured underpants.

'The sight of a nude male surely can't be so shocking, can it? After all, there was Paul ... the two of you were married, even if you are claiming that his death made you frigid. You must have known what boys look like.'

The hint of teasing in his voice made her skin burn. She was too stunned to correct his mistaken assumption that her frigidity was the result of Paul's death. 'Boys, yes, but ... but you aren't a boy, Gray.'

He didn't say anything, but Stephanie had the distinct impression that he smiled faintly before he pulled his shirt on.

Watching his fingers move deftly over the buttons, securing them so that the tanned expanse of his torso with its shadowing of dark silk hair was hidden from her, aroused the most curious sensation in the pit of her stomach. He walked over to his dresser and pulled out a set of cuff-links.

'Damn, I can't seem to manage these. Come and give me a hand will you, Steph?'

Numbly she walked over to him, trying to focus her eyes on the sinewed strength of his wrist as he bared it for her inspection. The contrast between his dark, tanned skin and the crisp whiteness of his shirt cuff was curiously disturbing. She wanted to put her fingertips over the strong pulse she could see beating under his skin, and feel its heat. She wanted the comfort and security of his arms, in the same way she had wanted them when Paul was killed.

It seemed to take a lifetime to secure both cuff-links,

but at last it was done. When she stepped back from him she was surprised to see how shaky she felt.

'I'd better go down and check on dinner.'

As she stepped away from him, Stephanie thought she heard him laugh softly.

What was happening to her? she wondered numbly as she went downstairs. She already knew she was sexless, incapable of arousing a man, so why was she so suddenly and inexplicably experiencing this odd desire to reach out and touch Gray? She had been shocked and embarrassed by his nudity but she had felt something else as well: a purely feminine recognition of the powerful masculinity of him, an intensely female responsiveness to his maleness. But surely that was impossible? She couldn't experience those sort of feelings. Could she?

Thoroughly confused, she tried to concentrate on preparing their meal, and to direct her thoughts to whatever it was that Gray wanted to discuss with her, but irrationally they kept straying to Gray's earlier assertion that he wasn't qualified to judge whether she was frigid or not.

Could Paul have been wrong? She frowned. But surely if he had been she would have known about it before now? In the ten years since his death she had never once experienced the slightest desire for any man. The phone rang, and she went to answer it.

It was Carla, asking for Gray. As she called him to the phone Stephanie was gripped by the most painfully acute sensation of jealousy. Jealousy? But she had no right to be jealous of Carla's place in Gray's life. No right at all.

Thoroughly confused, she went back to the kitchen, trying to dismiss her painfully intrusive thoughts.

When he came into the kitchen Gray was frowning heavily. Whatever Carla had had to say to him it couldn't have been to his liking. Had the blonde perhaps objected to *her* presence at the cottage, after all? If Gray was *her* lover ... *Gray* her *lover*? Shock ripped through her unprepared body—the body she was so convinced could never respond sexually to any man. What on earth was happening to her?

'Stephanie ... what is it? Are you ill?'

She looked up, her eyes still dark with shock. She opened her mouth to speak, but no words emerged. She was looking at Gray and yet it was almost as though she was looking at a stranger.

He reached out for her, warm hands gripping her rigid arms, his face creased in lines of concern.

'You're trembling. What is it? What's wrong?'

Another minute and she would be cradled against the hard warmth of his body ... the body that, like the man, belonged to someone else. Immediately she tensed, and Gray let her go.

She felt sick with shock as she realised what she was feeling. She was jealous. Jealous of Carla. No, not of Carla, she amended hastily ... she was jealous of their relationship, because it threatened her own friendship with Gray. Yes, that was it ...

Shakily she let her mind absorb her thoughts, like a swimmer frightened by the depths, now reaching out for the safety of the shallows where they could touch the ocean floor.

'I'm all right now, Gray ...'

It was obvious that he wasn't totally convinced. 'What happened?'

She shrugged carelessly. 'Oh, nothing. I just felt cold, that's all.'

It was plain that he didn't believe her, but fortunately he didn't press the subject.

'I'll fix the trays. Will you check on the casserole?'

Everything was as it had always been, she thought thankfully, obeying his instructions. Or was it? She risked a covert glance at him. She was terrified of losing his friendship . . . especially to another woman.

CHAPTER TWO

THEY had eaten both the casserole and the apple pie before Gray broached the subject of Stephanie's visit.

'I'll wash up if you make the coffee,' he suggested, bending to take the tray from her lap. 'No one else makes it quite the way you do.'

'Oh, no? I'll bet you say that to all the girls.'

Instead of making him smile, her flip answer drew a sharp frown. Now what had she done to offend him? she wondered unhappily as she followed him to the kitchen. Something was different; something had changed between them. She felt different than she had ever felt before, buoyed up and excited one moment, and miserable and on edge the next.

Amazingly, Gray managed to unfasten his cuff-links much more easily than she had put them in. Watching him as he rolled up his shirt-sleeves and started washing up their dishes, Stephanie felt a burning tide of awareness sweep over her body. His forearms were tanned and strongly muscled. She wanted to reach out and touch him, to stroke her fingertips through those thick, dark hairs.

'I asked you to come down here because I need a favour.' The abrupt words cut through the hazy sensuality of her private thoughts, jerking her back to reality. What on earth had come over her?

'I'm having some problems with the boat-yard.

Business has fallen off quite sharply lately. I'm working on the design for a new boat which I'm hoping will be successful. If all goes well I plan to show it at next year's Boat Show, but launching a new boat is a pretty risky business, especially for a yard like ours.'

For no reason at all, a cold spiral of fear had invaded the pit of her stomach. Gray had stopped washing the dishes and had turned round to face her. The atmosphere in the kitchen was tense, almost stiflingly so.

'I'm entering this year's Fastnet, Steph,' Gray told her quietly. 'If I can win, and I think I can, the publicity would give the new boat a boost that nothing else could match. Winning the Fastnet will give us more publicity, more credibility than we could get from any amount of advertising.'

Stephanie knew that every word he said was true. A boat designed and made by an acknowledged winner of a race as prestigious as the Fastnet would sell better than a tennis racquet endorsed by a Davis Cup champion, but nothing could silence the words of protest from tumbling from her lips. Since Paul's death she had been left with a morbid fear of the sea. She knew that he was himself to blame for the accident by his rash disregard of the safety rules, that did not quell her fear, there was more to it than that.

She could hardly bear to look at the sea, even on a calm day and, as Gray well knew, coming down here to the estuary was purgatory for her.

She had once loved sailing. It was her father's hobby and, like him, she had been thrilled about his transfer to this part of the coast which had a reputation of being an idyllic spot for small boat enthusiasts.

She had been more grateful than she could say when her father had been transferred to an inland posting shortly after Paul's death, and never once since that time had she set foot in a boat herself, even though she had once crewed enthusiastically and knowledgeably both for her father, and for Paul.

Now Gray was telling her that he intended to enter one of the most dangerous races of all, and she shook with fear for him.

'Gray . . . please don't,' she pleaded huskily.

'Stephanie, I have to. Don't you understand?' he demanded harshly. 'If I don't, I stand to lose the boat-yard . . . I have no other choice.'

She could see that, but she still longed to beg him to change his mind. Instead, she said shakily, 'Gray, please . . . I don't want to lose you as well.'

'You won't, I promise you you won't.' She felt him move as he gathered her against his body, bracing himself against the unit as he rocked her gently in his arms.

Tense with fear, Stephanie buried her face against his chest, soothed by the heavy thud of his heart.

'If I'm to go ahead I'm going to need your help, Steph.' His voice was muffled slightly by her hair, and slightly unsteady, as though he was under a tremendous strain. 'I want you to move into the cottage, and take over the day-to-day running of the boat-yard for me until after the race. You could work from here on your illustrations, just as easily as you do in London . . .'

'Run the yard!' She jerked away from him, horrified. 'I couldn't do that.'

'Yes, you could. You did it when you and Paul were married.'

It was true that she had helped out at the yard all those years ago, organising the office along more practical lines.

'Stephanie, when have I ever asked you for anything?' His voice was rough, grating against her tense nerves. It was true, in their relationship he had always been the giver, she the taker. Although he didn't say it, she felt that he was reminding her that she owed him a debt—a debt he was now calling in. How could she explain to him how much she feared and loathed everything that reminded her of Paul? He thought she was still grieving for a husband she had loved and adored. How could she tell him that what she felt was guilt—that there was no love ... that the reality of marriage had woken her from what had only been an adolescent's dream?

'I ... I need time to think ...' Implicit in her husky words was an acknowledgement of all that she owed him.

He had stood by her when she felt everyone else was against her, accusing her of pushing Paul to his death, because of their quarrel. How could she deny his request for help? She knew how much the boat-yard meant to him.

Almost on a sigh she heard herself saying, 'I ... I've made up my mind. I'll do it ... I ...'

She didn't get the opportunity to say any more. She was in Gray's arms, held tight in a crushing grip that drove the breath from her lungs and brought a surge of blind panic as her body remembered how often it had been imprisoned with similar force by Paul.

She fought frantically against his constraining hold, until she felt him releasing her. Breathing deeply, she staggered back against the wall, her eyes dark with fear.

'For God's sake! What the hell did you think I was going to do ... Rape you?'

As she raised her shocked eyes to his, Stephanie saw him rake angry fingers through his hair.

'I know how you feel about Paul, Stephanie, but you can't cling to those memories for ever. Christ, if that's how you react when someone else touches you, I'm not surprised there hasn't been anyone else.'

The look in his eyes chilled her, she felt like a child abandoned by its parents, and longed to cry out to him to understand.

Instead she moved away from the wall, and turned away, shivering with the inner bleakness possessing her.

'Stephanie . . .' She felt his fingers touch her arm and this time she didn't move away.

'Look, I'm sorry. We're both wound up. I should have remembered how much you hate being touched.'

Her expression gave her away and he grimaced wryly.

'Did you think I didn't know? You freeze every time I come near you.'

Did she?

'Has it ever occurred to you that there's something dangerously obsessive about your determination to remain faithful to Paul's memory? Do you think he would have done the same if the positions had been reversed?' he demanded harshly. 'It's time to put the past behind you, Steph. Nothing's going to bring Paul back. You've got to start learning to live again. You told me not long ago that you were frigid.' His hand slid to her face cupping it, lifting it so that he could look down into her eyes.

'I don't think you are, but I think you've convinced yourself of it because it makes it easier for you to escape from the pain of loving anyone else. It's easier to tell yourself you're frigid than to risk loving someone whom you might ultimately lose.'

She wanted to tell him that he was wong, that she *was* frigid, that Paul himself had told her so; but somehow she was mesmerised by the magnetic glitter of his eyes as his head bent slowly towards her own.

Slowly, shockingly she realised what he meant to do, and by the time that knowledge had infiltrated her brain it was too late to move away. His lips were moving gently and softly over her own, their commanding impact making hers cling bemusedly to his warmth. Shock held her unmoving within his embrace, her breath obstructed by what was happening to her. She could feel her heart racing.

'Stay with me, Stephanie. Stay with me and help me . . .' Gray whispered the words against her mouth, and they brought her back to reality, releasing her from the trance imposed by his totally unexpected kiss. She drew away shakily and he let her, watching her through half-closed eyes.

'Yes . . . Yes, I will.' Her lips framed the words slowly, still quivering from the silken pressure of Gray's kiss. Thoroughly bemused, she was barely aware of what she was saying. She heard him laugh softly, deep in his throat, as he stepped back from her.

'You kiss like a little girl, do you know that?'

Pain pierced her. What on earth was she thinking of? To let Gray kiss her? And as for Gray himself . . . Her claim that she was frigid must have piqued his male curiosity, but now he knew the truth for himself he was hardly likely to kiss her again, she reflected flatly, still trying to recover from the blow of his soft-voiced taunt.

Her pride demanded some recompense and so, turning her back on him and busying herself with the coffee, she said coolly, 'We're friends, Gray, not lovers, and that's how I kissed you—as a friend.'

She was a little surprised by the anger in his eyes when he reached past her to relieve her of the heavy coffee jug. She and Gray had often had arguments in the past and he had never seemed to harbour any resentment on those occasions when she won. In fact, Gray had always encouraged her to think for herself and to form her own views. He had never been the sort of man who preferred women to be obedient, quiet echoes of their men's views.

'If I'm going to stay on to look after the yard I'll need to go back to London to collect my paints and some extra clothes.'

'I'll run you back on Monday morning. I've got some business to deal with, so I'll stay at your place Monday night and then we'll come back together on Tuesday. I'm not going to give you any opportunity to back out of this, Steph,' he warned her, before she could speak. 'I need your help too much for that.'

He wasn't saying so but Stephanie also knew that he had every right to ask for and expect her help. He had, after all, given her his in those dark months after the accident. Without his support ... She shuddered slightly, remembering the accusations she had flung at him then; the demand that he leave her to simply die. There had been plenty of times when she hadn't wanted to go on living, when she had thought that there was no longer any point to life, but Gray had refused to let her go, to let her abandon herself to that sort of self-destruction.

Yes, she owed him a lot, but how on earth was she going to cope with living so close to the sea; with knowing that every day Gray himself was out there, sailing on it; that Gray was going to enter one of the most dangerous sailing races in the world? The cup she was holding slid from her fingers to crash down on to the stone floor, her hands going up to cover her face.

In a tortured voice she pleaded, 'Gray, please don't do it! There must be another way.'

Tough, work-scarred fingers pulled her hands away from her eyes so that he could look at her.

'I have to do it,' he told her grimly. '*Can't* you understand that? The yard's been losing money steadily over the last few years—you know that ...'

She had, of course, but she had not realised how intensely Gray was worrying about it.

'There's still money coming in from the moorings you let out to summer visitors.'

'Yes, they're just about keeping us afloat, but it's not enough. I want this yard to be again what it once was. There's no cash available for development and invest-ment ... to do the things I want to do. You know that the design and production of small craft has always been more important to me than the day-to-day running of the yard.'

'But the Fastnet . . .' she protested weakly. 'Gray . . . What . . . what does Carla think about it?'

The words were out before she could stop them. A curious expression, half-pain, half-pride, crossed Gray's face.

'She knows that it's something I have to do,' he told her quietly, and she was pierced with a poignant sense of loss, so totally did his voice and expression exclude her.

In those few words Gray had condemned her to the periphery of his life; had shown her that there was someone else in his life far more important to him than she could ever be.

She swallowed hard against the pain.

'You love her a great deal.' Her voice trembled and she saw Gray's brief smile.

'Can one quantify love? I don't think so.'

'Did you know the moment you met her that . . .?'

'That I had found the woman I was going to love for the rest of my life?' he submitted for her.

Something quivered and hurt inside her, some deep-lodged pain that, like a tiny splinter buried deep in one's flesh, festered and irritated. *Why* had she never known before how possessive she felt about Gray? *Why* had it taken another woman to open her eyes to how desirable a man he was?

'You're looking very pale. What's wrong?'

'I just don't like the thought of you entering the Fastnet.' It wasn't a lie, but it wasn't the entire truth either. It was the thought of losing him to Carla that had driven the blood from her face, just as much as the thought of losing him to the sea had frozen her heart in ice.

'Come and have a look at the plans, I've got them here in my study.'

Something in the firm purposefulness of his voice calmed her a little. Gray knew the sea . . . he did not take risks . . . he never had. She remembered how thrilled she had been on the rare occasions she had sailed with him. Even then he had been fascinated by the problems of designing safe racing craft. His uncle had called it time-wasting. He preferred the more mundane side of the business. He had wanted to sell off part of the boat-yard to form a huge marina, but Gray and the local council had opposed him, and rightly so. It would have completely spoiled the atmosphere of the small village.

Somehow she found herself being guided into the study and sitting down alongside Gray while he unrolled plans for the hull of the new racing craft.

Soon he was lost in enthusiasm for what he was doing, pointing out to her how the design could be modified to fit into a family market; how the utilitarian interior of the prototype racing craft could be turned into comfortably luxurious accommodation for a small family.

At the moment, Stephanie was working on the book cover for a novel set in the Caribbean, and in her mind's eye she saw Gray's sleek new craft swinging gently at anchor in the background.

For ten years she had turned her back completely on sailing but now, poring over the plans Gray had spread out on the large partners' desk in the study, she felt all the old enthusiasm and excitement of her teenage years come rushing back. A single glance had been enough to show her the grace and potential of Gray's new boat. Without even having to strain her imagination to the slightest degree, she could already see the boat's sleek lines as she sped over the water; she could almost feel the old thrill of racing against other small craft, the salt-laden breeze stinging her skin and lifting her hair. Those had been good days ... happy, carefree days, before ...

'These new compounds mean that we can make the hull lighter than ever before, and these sails——' Gray's finger indicated one of the sketches, and Stephanie pushed aside the past to concentrate on what he was showing her.

Unlike many of the entrants in the Fastnet Race, Gray's yacht would only be sailed by him. Apparently, the fact that it could be handled by one man alone was one of its potential selling points in its racier form.

'The sails will certainly give it plenty of speed,' Stephanie remarked.

Her fear must have shown in her voice, because Gray said lightly, 'Yes, and the special buoyancy tanks we've fitted will make it virtually unsinkable. The beauty of this design is that it can be fitted out as anything from a racing yacht to a sea-going cruiser, depending on what the customer wants. More and more people are sailing these days, and they're demanding a wider and better equipped range of craft at the right price. I need that business, Stephanie, and I'm determined to get it.' He rolled up the plans. 'So far we're very pleased with the way she's tested out. I'm hoping to do the final sea trials in the next couple of weeks.'

She shivered slightly, unaware of the way the light from the lamp highlighted the rich copper tone of her hair. In the last ten years she had changed from a pretty girl into a beautiful, although somewhat haunted woman, Gray thought, watching her. He had a momentary impulse to reach out and watch her hair glide through his fingers, to see if it felt as warm and vibrant as it looked. Her mouth curved as she smiled uncertainly at him, and he got up abruptly.

'You stay there, I'll go and make us both some coffee.'

The clipped way he spoke broke the mood of relaxed friendship between them. It was almost as though he didn't want her company ...

Stephanie turned her head to one side automatically, hiding her expression from him. It was idiotic to feel hurt, but they had been getting on so well, and then for no reason at all, or so it seemed, Gray had suddenly retreated from her.

After he had gone into the kitchen for their coffee, Stephanie hunched her arms round her knees. The light from the lamp illuminated the haunting pensiveness of her face. Gray was right, it was time she learned to come to terms with the past, but every time she thought about Paul, every time she remembered his cruel words, every time she remembered how quickly their love had died, pain engulfed her.

It was safer to love a man the way she loved Gray, as a brother, rather than to love one the way she had loved Paul. And yet ... She frowned, and chewed anxiously on her bottom lip. There was something different about Gray. She was aware of a tension within him that she had never noticed before. Gray was always so calm and controlled. She had rarely seen him lose his temper, never heard him raise his voice. He was a man of infinite resource and capability, adept at concealing his thoughts and his feelings, and yet today she had sensed that that control was slipping. Was it just because he was worried about the boat-yard?

She was still puzzling over a change in him when he came back with their coffee. A quick look at his face revealed that he was smiling at her, and Stephanie expelled a faint sigh of relief, without really knowing why she should do so. All she could think was that she didn't want to be at odds with Gray, whatever the reason, and yet in the past they had quarrelled mightily over various issues on which they had taken opposing stances without it damaging their relationship in the slightest. So why was she so afraid now? Was it perhaps because of Carla? Did she fear that she might lose his friendship? That somehow his relationship with Carla threatened his relationship with her? But surely that was silly; she and Gray were friends, Carla and Gray were lovers.

'Penny for them?'

Instinctively she bent her head so that a silky swathe of hair hid her expression from him. It was the first time she had ever felt the need to be defensive with Gray, and part of her mourned the fact that this should be so.

'They aren't worth it.' She smiled up at him and wondered if her smile looked as forced as it felt. 'I think I'll go up to bed, if you don't mind, Gray. I'm tired—it must be the hot weather.'

She had to avoid looking at him as she gave voice to the small lie. She never went to bed early on the first night of her visits. She and Gray normally stayed up until the early hours of the morning, catching up on one another's news, teasing each other, talking ... But tonight, for some reason, she was conscious of an air of constraint between them, and almost every time she looked at Gray, she couldn't help mentally picturing him with Carla, his body as magnificently nude as it had been earlier, its muscled hardness covering the blonde's more delicately female shape.

Gray didn't say a word about her unusual decision to go to bed early, but as he walked her to the door and opened it for her, Stephanie glanced up at him and saw that his dark eyebrows were drawn together in a heavy frown.

Instinctively, without thinking what she was doing, she raised herself up on tiptoe, and pressed her fingertips to the frown lines, tenderly smoothing them away. Her gesture was completely unselfconscious, born of her desire to restore their relationship to its normal footing, but from the way Gray reacted her touch might have burned his skin like acid.

Lean fingers clamped round her wrist, his head jerking back as though he loathed the physical contact between their skins.

The pain of his bone-crunching grip was nothing to compare with the anguish of rejection which Stephanie suffered, when she saw the look of revulsion in his eyes.

'Gray!' Shock rounded her eyes to deep violet pools of pain, humiliation sending a burning wave of scarlet across her skin. Her arm throbbed from the tightness of his grip, and a terrible feeling of nausea churned in her stomach. What was it she had done?

Blue eyes narrowed sharply on her face, a hard burn of colour darkening the taut thrust of Gray's cheekbones. More than ever he reminded her of a beast of prey, a dangerous jungle cat, waiting to pounce on its victim.

'What did I do wrong?'

The words whispered past lips trembling slightly with the aftermath of shock.

Stephanie saw Gray's lips twist. 'Twenty-eight years old and you have to ask me that? You haven't done the male sex any favours by living like a nun since Paul's death, Steph.'

The violet eyes betrayed bewilderment and he made a sound of self-derision deep in his throat, caught midway between anger and amusement.

'For God's sake, do you want me to spell it out for you?'

Something dangerous had been let loose in the room: Stephanie could sense it and yet she didn't know where the danger came from. She touched the tip of her tongue to her trembling lips, moistening them, in an acutely nervous gesture, blinking a little as she saw the flat hardness compressing Gray's mouth as he watched her movements like a hawk.

Her voice in a husky whisper she protested, 'Gray, I only touched you. I've touched you before.'

'Now it's different.' His voice was flat, metallic almost, as though he'd deliberately forced every iota of emotion out of it. 'Then I wasn't suffering from the frustration that's eating into me now.'

The shock of it tensed her muscles. Gray had never spoken to her like this before, never mentioned his physical desires, or the women he shared them with.

She wet her lips again, conscious of a strange heat burning through her veins. She didn't want to hear about Gray's sex life, but for some reason she heard herself saying slowly, 'Carla . . .?'

'Carla's married, Steph.'

Numb with shock, Stephanie heard him swear. For some reason her heart was racing, her nerve-endings pulsingly conscious of Gray's tension. She saw him move and stiffened with shock as his fingers bit into the tender flesh of her upper arms.

'You don't even know what I'm talking about, do you?' His voice was thick and unfamiliar, and for the first time since she had known him, his movements were less than perfectly controlled. She could actually hear the fierce thud of his heart as he closed the distance between them, so loud that it drowned her instinctive gasp of shock.

'This is what it's all about, Stephanie. This, and this.' He pulled her so close to his body that she could feel its heat; so close that, shockingly, she was aware of his physical arousal. If just the thought of Carla could affect him like this . . . Icy cold with shock, she shuddered. Instantly Gray released her, an expression of cold withdrawal icing over his eyes.

'I'm sorry.' His voice was curt. 'I shouldn't have done that.'

He turned his back to her, and part of her ached to reach out and comfort him. Instead she said shakily. 'It's all right, Gray. I . . . I . . . understand. At least, I think I do.'

'Do you?' He turned to look at her, searching her face

with hard eyes. Stephanie made herself hold that searching gaze.

'I think so. You love Carla, but she's married to someone else. You love someone who's out of reach.'

'I certainly do.' The look he gave her was wryly sardonic. 'Go to bed, Stephanie,' he told her tiredly. 'I don't think there's any point in discussing things any further.'

Despite her original claim that she was tired, Stephanie couldn't sleep. It had come as a shock to learn that Gray was in love with Carla, and it hadn't been a pleasant shock. In fact, she was stunned to discover just how resentful and unhappy she felt. She loved him as a friend, as a brother—so why did she feel like this?

Of course, it was because Carla was married. That was the explanation! Poor Gray, what a terrible situation for him. She knew how devastating jealousy could be, and he *must* be jealous of Carla's husband— jealous and frustrated. Her face burned as she remembered the way he had demonstrated that frustration to her. She had never known Gray behave with anything other than calm, brotherly affection; had never before seen him like this, driven, and almost aggressive towards her. She hated the thought of their relationship changing; of another woman coming between them.

She told herself she was being unrealistic, selfish even, but it didn't help.

'I'm sorry about last night—things got a little out of control.' Gray grimaced faintly as he handed Stephanie her breakfast. 'I don't normally let go like that.'

He was watching her covertly, as though expecting

... expecting what? Despite her own complicated feelings last night, Stephanie had made a vow that she would give Gray all the emotional support she could to sustain him during what she knew from her own experience would be a very traumatic time.

'Carla's husband and I are financial partners in the boat I'm sailing for the Fastnet—that's how I met her.'

Stephanie knew that her disquiet must have shown in her eyes, because Gray's mouth twisted. 'We can't *all* love to order,' he told her, curtly turning away from her. 'We'll leave for London this afternoon to collect your stuff. We'll stay at your place overnight.'

'You'll have to sleep on the settee,' she warned him.

'It won't matter for one night, and besides, I'd never get an hotel room at this time of year.'

'No. London is packed with tourists. Have you much business to do?'

Gray shook his head, pouring them both a second cup of coffee. 'No, I should be through it by lunchtime, and then we can head back here in the afternoon. By the way, you'll need a room to work in while you're here. There's an empty office down at the yard, will that do? I could show you it later.'

This was more like the Gray she knew, and although it hurt her that he didn't want to discuss Carla with her, part of her was glad. She was growing to hate the sound of the other woman's name.

She thought she'd been successful in keeping her thoughts hidden from him until he said softly, 'What is it, Steph?'

'I'm worried about you—about your involvement with Carla.'

For some reason her admission alarmed her, and she looked down at her plate, missing the look of brooding pain he gave her.

'Why?'

'I don't know. Perhaps it's because I know you're not the sort of man who'd really want to be involved with a woman who's married to someone else,' she offered lamely. 'You're always so honest in everything you do, Gray.'

'Think you know me well, don't you? Well, don't be too sure, love. The pain of an almost unendurable physical desire that you know can never really be satisfied makes a man do irrational things. Remember that, Steph.'

What was he trying to tell her? A faint shiver of apprehension held her in a cold grip. Instinctively she reached out to cover his hand with her own. His hands were large and well shaped with long fingers, clever hands . . . caring hands.

'Does she feel the same way about you, Gray? Will she . . .?' She swallowed, knowing it hurt to say what she had to say. 'Will she leave her husband for you?'

'No to both questions. Alex is a very wealthy man. Carla would never leave him.'

Her heart ached with pain for him, her huge eyes violet-shadowed with the intensity of her emotions. Wanting to offer him comfort, she moved closer to him, leaning her head against his shoulder and placing her hand against his chest. The neck of his shirt was open and her fingertips accidentally grazed against his warm skin. Instantly, hot colour flooded her face as she remembered how she had seen him yesterday. Shocked by her mental picture of his nude body she started to move away, but Gray's hand clamped down over hers, imprisoning it against his chest. The sensation of bone and muscle moving beneath her palm was faintly unnerving.

She hadn't touched a man voluntarily since Paul's death. 'Give her up, Gray,' she pleaded softly, trying to drag her thoughts away from the strange tension that seemed to have sprung up between them. 'Stop seeing her.'

'I can't.' His voice was harsh, his chest rising sharply as though he was finding it hard to breathe. When she looked up into his face it was closed and set, his nostrils slightly flared. He looked like a man in the grip of a fierce and unwanted emotion. 'Alex is financing me in the Fastnet,' he told her starkly. 'Without him I couldn't even contemplate entering it. He's provided the money for the new ketch we'll be using. I've built her, and we've got a first-rate crew of local volunteers. I can't stop seeing her, Steph, not without making Alex suspicious.'

Stephanie shivered. 'It must be awful to love someone so much and know that you'll always be apart.'

'Awful?' Derision grated through the word. 'It's hell on earth!'

Stephanie looked up at him, shocked by the bitter intensity in his voice. His mouth curved in an unfamiliarly hard line. He had a very nice mouth, she thought absently, the top lip firmly drawn, the bottom one fuller.

As though it possessed a will beyond her control, her hand lifted, her fingertip gently touching that full bottom lip. She felt Gray tense, his fingers fastening round her wrist, his eyes furiously dark, as he looked down into the surprised violet innocence of her own.

'What the . . .?'

'I'm sorry, Gray.' Her eyes clouded, confusion spreading through her, almost as though she spoke the words for herself rather than him. She said huskily, 'I don't know why I did that . . . I just thought how nice your mouth was.' She frowned, breaking off incoherently. 'I . . .'

'It's OK.'

The anger was gone from his voice and she looked at him in relief. The expression in his eyes was shielded from her by twin fans of thick, dark lashes. She had always known that Gray was an attractive man, but until now she hadn't realised how attractive. The temptation to reach out and touch his lashes in the same way she had touched his mouth was almost too much for her. While she was still grappling with the strangeness of it, the dark lashes lifted and for a moment dark blue eyes looked relentlessly into vulnerable violet.

'It's all right if you want to touch me, Steph. I'm just not used to it, that's all. You're not a very touching person, are you?'

Wasn't she? Gravely she considered it.

She looked back at Gray, trying to interpret the expression in his eyes, but he veiled them from her, turning his head.

The sudden brief contact of his lips against the soft tips of her fingers in a butterfly kiss sent quivers of sensation racing from her nerve-endings, but before she could analyse why she should be so shocked, he was releasing her, and standing up.

'Come on. It's time we set off for the yard.'

As she moved past him towards the open door he watched her with an expression in his eyes that would have shocked her to the depths of her soul had she seen it. It was the look of a hungry, aching man fighting to hold on to his self-control.

Eleven years he had wanted her, from the day she had turned seventeen. She only had to touch him for him to go up in flames. When he had looked down at her and seen her looking at his mouth . . . God, but he had come close to betraying himself. She didn't have the slightest idea how he felt about her, and she never would, but sometimes the strain of maintaining their sexless friendship when he wanted . . . He swallowed hard, trying not to let himself imagine what it would be like to have her softness in his arms, to bury himself in her and love her in all the ways he ached to do. It was utterly pointless yearning for her; she loved Paul and she always would, he knew that. He had tried every way he knew how to stop loving her, to stop aching for her and wanting her, but none of them worked. It didn't matter how many other women he took to bed, in the end there was only her.

There were times when he almost wanted to take hold of her and *make* her respond to him; when he was almost driven mad by the torment of having her so close to him and yet so unattainable.

The day he knew he loved her, he had planned to wait until she had grown a little, until she knew enough about life to make her own decisions; but Paul had beaten him to it, Paul who had never waited for anything in his life, Paul who had seen the way his older cousin watched Stephanie's slender, copper-haired figure; Paul who had deliberately and knowingly taken her from him.

Grimacing faintly as he fell in step behind her, Gray reflected that it was just as well that she believed he loved Carla. He would have to have a word with Carla. She and Alex adored one another ... she had also guessed, in that infuriatingly intuitive way that women have, how he felt about Stephanie. In fact, the only person who didn't seem to know was Stephanie herself.

He shouldn't have given in to his own weakness and asked her to come down here. How on earth was he supposed to concentrate on working for the Fastnet, with Stephanie providing a constant distraction, a constant torment? A muscle beat betrayingly in his jaw as his body tensed. God, when she walked into his bedroom yesterday ... He had had to to turn away from her so that she wouldn't see. How on earth he had managed to get his body under control before it betrayed him, he still didn't know.

For one split second he had almost been on the point of begging her to touch him.

'Gray?'

Stephanie turned to wait for him to catch up with her. Under his tan, his face looked strained, and she ached to comfort him. She hated seeing him like this, but not as much as she hated the cause of his pain. How could Carla do this to him? Had she no compassion? But if Carla was free to marry Gray ... Stephanie shivered, knowing that she didn't want the other woman to have such a permanent place in Gray's life. She told herself that she wasn't jealous, that there was no reason for her to be, but knowing that Gray loved someone else somehow disturbed her.

CHAPTER THREE

THE ESTUARY was on one of the prettiest parts of the Channel coastline, and although Stephanie couldn't quite repress a shudder as they walked into the boatyard, part of her couldn't help being aware of what an attractive picture the variety of boats made as they clustered around the marina just beyond the yard.

Out in the mouth of the estuary where it joined the sea, a dinghy race was taking place, and she paused automatically to watch them tack in and out of the buoys, remembering how much pleasure she had once gained from sailing.

She had learned to sail almost as soon as she could walk, and she and her parents had spent many happy holidays indulging their love of the sport.

Since Paul's death, she hadn't set foot in a boat of any kind, and linked with her deep guilt over his death was her own almost phobic dread of anything connected with the sea.

'You've got quite a lot of work in hand,' she commented to Gray as she walked at his side.

He shrugged. 'Repairs mostly, and they don't bring in an awful lot. I've taken on an agency for one of the national small yacht builders, and that brings a reasonable amount in commission, but it isn't enough.'

He left her for a moment to go over and speak to the two men working on an upturned hull.

The clean, salty tang of sea air assailed her nostrils.

Almost against her will, Stephanie found her gaze drawn to the far horizon. It was a perfect day for sailing, just enough brisk wind . . .

'Fancy going out?'

She hadn't heard Gray coming back and she jumped, shocked that he could even make such a suggestion when he knew how she felt about the sea. She shook her head, and felt his fingers bite deeply into her arm.

'Paul's dead, Stephanie,' he told her harshly. 'Nothing's going to bring him back. Sooner or later you're going to have to face up to that fact and start re-building your own life. You've been living in a vacuum since he died,' he accused roughly. 'You've got to . . .'

He broke off, his eyes narrowing as a car drove into the yard.

Stephanie turned to look at it, and her heart plummeted as she saw Carla stepping out of the passenger seat of a racy-looking Jaguar car.

'Hi, there . . .'

The other woman was an excellent actress, she acknowledged grudgingly. No one could have guessed from the way she was smiling to include them both that she and Gray were anything other than merely friends.

A tall, fair-haired man extricated himself from the driver's seat of the car and put his arm round her shoulders. He was older than Gray, somewhere in his forties, but lean and bronzed and very fit-looking.

'That's Alex, Carla's husband,' Gray murmured to her.

For some reason she found that she was moving closer to him, almost as though she wanted to protect him. *Her*, protect Gray? She grimaced to herself as the other couple came over to them.

'Alex darling, I don't think you've met Stephanie before, have you?' Carla introduced.

Alex Farlow's handshake was as firm as Stephanie had anticipated it would be. He did not look like a man whose wife was being unfaithful to him, and Carla certainly did not look like a woman who was cheating on her husband. Her arm was tucked through his and she was smiling up at him in a teasing, loving way, that made Stephanie unable to look at Gray, standing so tensely at her side.

This must be purgatory for him, to see Carla with her husband, playing the part of a loving wife.

'No, we haven't met before.' Alex Farlow smiled. 'But I certainly have heard a lot about you, Stephanie.' He grinned at Gray as he spoke, and to Stephanie's astonishment she saw a dull burn of dark colour stain Gray's cheekbones. Gray was embarrassed ... but why ...?

'See, I told you that Gray wouldn't be in the mood for work today,' Carla announced, smiling up at her husband.

'We're on our way to Southampton, and I just thought I'd call in to tell you that a guy from *Yacht Owner* will be coming down to interview you about the new boat—that should give us some good publicity.'

The two men talked for a while about the progress on the boat, but then Carla tugged her husband away, exclaiming playfully, 'Alex, Gray doesn't often get the chance to spend time with Stephanie, and I'm sure he doesn't want to waste any of it talking boats ...'

Stephanie frowned as Carla drew her husband away. What was she trying to imply? That *she* and Gray were more than merely friends? Why? Did Alex perhaps suspect her relationship with Gray?

There had certainly been nothing remotely lover-like in their attitude to one another that she could see, and yet she couldn't help noticing that Gray was quick to detach Carla from her husband's side, as he walked with them towards their car. While Alex eased himself into the driver's seat, Carla and Gray stood talking, their voices too low for her to catch what they were saying, their heads close together. The pain inside her startled her. She was jealous . . . jealous of Carla! She shivered and told herself it was just the freshening breeze but, as Gray waved off the departing couple and came back to her, she felt as though somehow the brightness of the day had been inexplicably dimmed.

Gray took her into the office. Nothing had changed; the same old battered filing cabinets, the same ancient typewriter. The paperwork generated by the business was minimal and shouldn't take too much of her time.

She saw Gray glance at his watch.

'The new boat will have to wait for another time. We'd better get moving if we're going to collect your stuff.'

He was right. He was also withdrawn and almost distant with her, and her throat ached with compassion for him. Carla's brief appearance had done this to him.

She reached out to touch his arm, and immediately he tensed, frowning down at her.

'Gray, is there nothing I can do to help?' she asked him awkwardly.

For a moment she thought he was actually going to deny knowing what she meant, but then his frown eased slightly to be replaced by an expression of such bitter cynicism that she could have cried for him.

'It's no good. She'll never leave Alex. I know that now.'

Stephanie bit her lip. It was wrong of her to feel so relieved, but she couldn't help it. That must have been what they were talking about. Carla must have told him their affair was over. Odd, but she hadn't struck Stephanie as the type of woman to indulge in casual affairs. If she hadn't known better, on this morning's showing she would have judged her as a woman who was deeply in love and perfectly happy with her husband.

'They've got two children ... both boys ... They're away at boarding school but ...'

Stephanie pressed his arm in mute sympathy.

'Did you really mean what you said about ... about wanting to help?'

Gray's voice seemed to have become unfamiliarly thick. She glanced up at him, and saw that his skin was slightly flushed. It tore at her heart to see him looking so vulnerable, to have him in need of her help instead of the other way round.

'Anything,' she told him softly, meaning it. 'You know that.'

His mouth twisted in a strange smile.

'It's hell on earth wanting a woman who doesn't want you. I need something or someone to strengthen my will-power ... to stop me from doing something crazy ... You could be that someone, Steph.'

For a moment she could do nothing but stare at him. When she did manage to speak, her voice was a muffled croak.

'Me ... but how?'

His mouth twisted again.

'By the oldest method in the book. You could pretend to be my lover . . .'

For a moment she was too shocked to speak.

'But that wouldn't stop you wanting her,' she said at last.

'No,' Gray agreed bleakly, 'but it would help to salvage my pride . . . and the boat-yard. Don't you see, Steph?' He grabbed hold of her arms, pulling her so close to him that she could see the dark irises of his eyes, the pupils enlarged with emotion and pain.

'Having you as my make-believe lover will erect a barrier between us. It will help to stop me from running after her and making a complete fool of myself. And it will stop Alex from finding out . . .'

'That you're in love with his wife.'

Why did saying the words cause her so much pain? She gnawed on her bottom lip, knowing there was no way in a hundred years she could play such a role convincingly.

As though he read her mind, Gray released her and stepped back from her.

'It's all right. I shouldn't have asked you. It's expecting too much to . . .'

'No!' Her own denial startled her. She gave a shaky laugh and went on. 'I *will* do it, Gray. I owe you that much—and more . . . much more than I can ever repay. But I'm not sure that I'll be very convincing.'

The pain in his eyes was almost too much for her. She felt her throat close up against the tears forming. She hurt for him.

He had his back to her, but there was no mistaking the sarcasm in his voice as he said cruelly, 'You can remember how it was with Paul though, can't you . . .?'

The pain of his words shut off her breath. She wanted to cry out against it, but the agony inside her was too great. She made a sound in her throat, something between a cry and a moan, and instantly Gray was at her side.

'Oh God, Steph. I'm sorry.' He was rocking her in his arms, holding her so closely that she could feel the heat coming off his skin, and instantly she remembered how it had felt to have the aroused pressure of his flesh against her own.

Immediately she tensed and recoiled from him, shocked by the surge of sensation engulfing her own body. She felt Gray release her, his expression shuttered as he looked down at her.

'I'm sorry.' His voice was clipped. 'I didn't mean to hurt you.'

And she wasn't sure if he meant physically or emotionally.

They set out for London and Stephanie's flat after a snack lunch. Gray was driving his Range Rover. It was a pleasant change to make the journey with some degree of comfort. Her VW wasn't designed for long journeys.

Conversation between them was desultory. Stephanie asked about his progress with the development of the new boat and how he and Alex intended to market it. There was a constraint between them that had not been there before, and when at last they were on the outskirts of the city, Gray said curtly, 'Look, if you want to change your mind and recall your offer of help, you only have to say so.'

'I don't,' Stephanie told him quietly. 'Unless, of course, *you're* having second thoughts.'

A muscle twitched betrayingly in his jaw as he clenched his teeth and Stephanie knew how much it must be costing him to go through with the farce of pretending he no longer loved the other woman.

'There'll be a certain amount of talk—gossip about us,' he warned her. 'It's unavoidable, living in such a small place.'

Stephanie was startled. 'Why should there be? Everyone knows . . .'

'That you're still mourning the death of your husband,' he jeered unkindly. 'Stephanie, that was ten years ago. You're an adult woman and you'll be living under the roof of an equally adult male. People are bound to jump to conclusions.'

'I've stayed with you before and . . .'

'This time it's different,' Gray interrupted.

Stephanie had lived in London for too long to be concerned about the threat of unfounded gossip. She shrugged her shoulders. 'Does it really matter what people think? You and I . . .'

Gray looked at her. 'Well, if *you're* not concerned, I don't suppose there's any reason why I should be. I just thought I'd warn you.'

'That people will look on me as your live-in lover?' She shrugged again. 'I can't believe that that's going to occasion much gossip these days!'

She glanced across at Gray and was surprised to see that he was frowning as though for some reason her comment displeased him. Was he secretly still hoping that Carla would change her mind, and was this the reason for his reticence?

She felt unable to question him too closely on a subject that was obviously intensely painful to him.

They reached her flat without incident, parking outside the Victorian villa in which it was situated. Stephanie's flat was on the top floor, where the attic windows had an excellent north light, ideal for her work.

The flat comprised a hall, sitting-room, dining kitchen, bathroom and two bedrooms, the smallest of which she used as a workroom and in which she had set up her easel and reference books, plus a desk and filing cabinet.

As she had already warned Gray, he would have to sleep on her rather small bed-settee.

Because she hadn't anticipated returning quite so soon, her fridge was empty, and Gray offered to go out and find them something to eat while she started to pack. She had taken the precaution of storing several heavy-duty cardboard boxes in the back of the Range Rover and Gray carried them upstairs for her, following her into her bedroom with them.

She had decorated the room herself in muted neutral shades, livened with a sunny yellow and deep blue, and Gray glanced round appreciatively, his eyes lingering briefly on the narrowness of her single bed before he commented drily, 'No frills and feminine furbelows, that's my Stephanie.'

For some reason his remark hurt her and she turned her back on him, snapping, 'I suppose Carla's bedroom is all pink and white with miles of lace!' And then she broke off, her face scarlet with mortification. What on earth had come over her? She bit her lip and looked uncertainly at Gray. 'I'm sorry, I . . .'

'I don't know what her room looks like,' he told her flatly. 'I've never been in it, but somehow I can't see

Alex having a taste for pink and white, can you?'

Oh God, how cruel of her, to remind him that the woman he loved did not sleep alone but shared her bed with her husband.

She went over to him, laying her hand on his arm. 'Gray . . .'

Immediately he jerked away from her.

'Save it,' he advised her curtly, opening the bedroom door. 'I'll go out and see what I can dig up in the way of food.'

After he had gone, Stephanie opened her wardrobe doors, and then stared blindly at the contents. How could she have hurt him like that? But she simply hadn't thought. She had been so . . . so hurt by his laconic comment about her bedroom that she had simply lashed out at him without thought.

But *why* had she been hurt? He had only spoken the truth. Why all of a sudden did she find her celibacy such a burden? Surely she had taught herself years ago to accept the fact that sexually she was a failure. Why now, of all times, did she have to start feeling like this?

Like what? she asked herself wryly. Like she was jealous of Carla . . . jealous of the fact that Gray loved and desired her? She had always known that Gray didn't live the life of a monk, why on earth should it only start to bother her now?

Perhaps because in the past Gray had never mentioned any of the women he was involved with, never introduced her to any of them, never intimated in any way at all that his mode of life was any different from her own.

Was she so damaged that she actually resented the closeness of others? Was that what was wrong with her?

Was she envious of Gray's ability to both give and receive the sexual fulfilment that had always been denied to her, or was her jealousy of a more intimate and dangerous nature?

Such as ... Immediately she stiffened, refusing to allow her thoughts free rein, flinging herself into a fever of activity to stop herself from pursuing trains of thought she knew instinctively would lead to danger.

Gray was gone less than half an hour, returning with a Chinese take-away which they ate in front of her sitting-room fire.

It was no longer possible to burn real fuel in the grate, but she had splurged on a very effective fake gas fire, which gave off both heat and the illusion of flickering flames.

'Good, but not as good as the real thing,' Gray commented, looking at it. 'But then, nothing ever is.'

There was something in his eyes as he looked at her that made her stomach churn with restless aching tension, although she didn't know what it was.

She looked away from him and got up clumsily. 'I'd better get these things washed up.'

'I'll do that. You carry on with your packing. I'd like an early start in the morning, if that's OK with you. We'll get all your stuff packed in the car tonight, and then we can leave right after breakfast.'

Stephanie had no objections to his plans and, while he washed up from their meal, she continued with her packing, leaving Gray to carry the heavy boxes downstairs and store them in his car.

By nine o'clock everything was in. Straightening her aching back, Stephanie grimaced. 'I don't know about you, but I'm whacked—and stiff as well.'

'A hot bath will get rid of that.' Gray glanced at his watch. 'You go and have one, I'll make us both a hot drink.'

There was no reason for her to feel self-conscious, and yet for some reason she did.

She felt far too on edge to linger in the bath, getting out and drying herself quickly, and then pulling on clean clothes.

Gray looked surprised when she emerged so quickly.

'I thought you'd have a good long soak. You still look very tense. Where is it sore? Here?' He reached out quite naturally, spreading his hand over her shoulder, his fingers gently massaging the back of her neck where the tension was the greatest.

For one weak moment she thought about relaxing against their stroking pressure; about closing her eyes and . . . Her eyelashes flickered and she felt the warmth of Gray's breath against her face as he bent towards her.

'You're losing weight.' His free hand cupped her face, pulling her round to face him, his thumb gently probing the shadow beneath her eye. 'I shouldn't have let you work so hard.'

A dangerous lassitude was creeping over her, an aching need to simply lean against Gray's strength both emotionally and physically.

'Gray . . .'

His hand slid into her hair, soothing away the tension locking her muscles. She closed her eyes, relaxed by the proximity of him where before she had been alarmed by it, her senses soothed by the familiar scent of him.

'What is it?'

She looked up to smile at him, and then suddenly remembered Carla.

When he held Carla in his arms, it would not be just to comfort her ... like a child.

Abruptly she pulled away from him, terrified of pursuing the thought any further. She was becoming almost obsessed by his relationship with the other woman. Her skin burned with the intimacy of her thoughts and she felt as guilty as though she had actually observed them making love. In her thoughts she *had* pictured the two of them together ... and to her that was almost as bad ... almost as much of an intrusion into their privacy.

'Gray ... I'm tired. I think I'll go straight to bed.'

He let her go without a word, but as she walked to her room she was conscious of him watching her ... conscious that somehow, by drawing away from him so abruptly, she had created a coldness between them that had not been there before.

CHAPTER FOUR

STEPHANIE was awake early, her sleep disturbed by a tension she couldn't put a name to, until consciousness flooded back and she remembered the events of the previous day.

Now, lying in her nun-like single bed, watching the grey dawn break over the London roofs, it seemed incredible that she had allowed Gray to persuade her to move back to the estuary—even if it was only temporarily. And worse still ... she shivered involuntarily as she remembered the additional folly she had agreed to.

She couldn't blame Gray for wanting to uphold his pride, nor for his fears that the boat-yard could become bankrupt if Carla's husband chose to withdraw his support, but how on earth could she have been stupid enough to agree to play the part of his new lover?

It seemed incredible. She was the least likely candidate for such a role, and she was sure she would never be able to play it convincingly. But she had given Gray her word.

Soberly she showered and dressed, knowing that there was no going back. She had given Gray a commitment and her pride would not allow her to withdraw from it.

A dry throat drove her into the kitchen in search of a cup of coffee.

Gray was still asleep, and she hastily averted her eyes from his bare torso, tanned and darkened with a covering of fine hair. Would it feel as silky as it looked? Shocked, she stared unseeingly at the filter coffee machine, wondering where on earth such an alien and dangerous thought had come from.

She had several minutes to wait for the coffee and she moved restlessly back to the door, her eyes drawn immediately to where Gray lay fast asleep on her bed-settee.

Although a reasonably respectable size, there was no way it was big enough for Gray. He dwarfed it, looking oddly youthful and almost vulnerable, with his dark hair untidy, and his eyes closed in sleep.

Long, dark lashes lay against the sharp rise of his cheekbones. He made a small sound and moved in his sleep, twisting the already dishevelled bedclothes round his lean body as he rolled over.

Something stronger than logic impelled her forwards until she was standing looking down at him.

Her heart was beating extraordinarily fast and she felt as though she were on the edge of some dizzyingly frightening discovery—and then Gray moved again, his eyes opening abruptly.

When he reached out and cupped the back of her head, she was too stunned to move. The smile he was giving her was like no other she had ever seen. It curled his mouth with a languid male appreciation of her as a woman that made her pulses pick up and race frantically. His eyes had closed again and he levered himself up slightly, pulling her down towards himself at the same time.

The sensation of his mouth moving against her own, the sleep-warm scent of his skin, the rough rasp of his night's growth of beard against her face were all things that should have jerked her out of his arms immediately, but somehow her senses refused to respond in that way. Instead she found herself melting against him, her mouth softening beneath the gentle pressure of his.

She might have gone on melting mindlessly if his hand hadn't suddenly strayed towards her breast. Instantly she tensed.

His eyes opened, widened as they saw her face, and then grew shuttered, leaving her in no doubt that he had had no idea whom he had been kissing. But *she* could quite easily imagine who he had hoped it had been! Pain, sharp and bitter, pulsed inside her.

'Stephanie.'

She knew from the tone of his voice what he was going to say, and suddenly she didn't want to hear the words; didn't want to hear him saying he thought she had been Carla.

'I've just made some coffee,' she told him, trying to control the tremor in her voice. 'Would you ... would you like some?'

She thought she saw an expression of pain darken his eyes but then it was gone, his mouth bleak, his voice devoid of all expression, drained like that of a man tired of fighting against impossible odds, as he accepted quietly.

'That would be fine. Thank you.'

'I didn't mean to wake you, but you did say you wanted an early start, and there's nothing to keep us here.'

Stephanie knew that she was babbling, just as she knew that for the first time that she could remember she felt uncomfortable with him. It had been a shock to feel his mouth moving against hers ... but it had been something more than shock that she had felt. And she tensed against remembering that dangerous softening, the yielding sensation that had spread through her body at the touch of his lips.

He had been kissing *Carla*, she reminded herself fiercely. Not her.

She took him his coffee, taking care not to look at his body as he sat up and straightened the bedclothes.

'You can look now,' he told her drily, destroying her hope that he was not aware of her discomfort. He was looking at her, his eyes cool and determined, and Stephanie swallowed nervously.

'Stephanie, I ...'

He was going to apologise for kissing her; she knew it! She stumbled into speech before he could do so, telling him huskily, 'I know you thought I was Carla. It ... it must be very frustrating to see so much of her, but to know that she ... that she prefers to stay with her husband ...'

Her cheeks were pink by the time she had finished. She had said far more than she intended, and she cursed herself for inadvertently bringing up a subject that could only cause Gray pain.

He was watching her with a peculiarly brilliant intensity that made her lose her thread and feel as though every muscle in her body was locked in some kind of unbreakable vice.

'Hellish frustrating,' he agreed flatly, refusing to let

her look away. 'Shall I prove to you how much?'

Shock hit her first, followed quickly by pain, and then fear. She was backing away from him even before she had had time to form any conscious decision.

As though he had looked into her mind and saw what haunted her there, his hand suddenly dropped away, his face changing.

'For God's sake, Stephanie,' he demanded savagely, 'you didn't think I was going to *hurt* you, did you?'

What could she say? She knew of course that Gray would never hurt her, but briefly, for that soul-tormenting moment in time, she had forgotten this was *Gray*, and remembered only that he was a man.

The fear that he would start questioning her drove her into saying petulantly. 'I'm not like you, Gray. I don't play those sort of games.'

Anger gave way to incomprehension as he continued to look at her.

'What do you mean? *I* don't play games, Steph. You should know me well enough for that.'

Her colour high, Stephanie said bleakly, 'I meant your remark about me ... about ...'

'About my physical frustration,' Gray supplied grimly, as realisation dawned. His mouth thinned as he said curtly, 'Don't worry about it, Steph. For a moment I forgot that you don't suffer the same feelings as the rest of us mortals.'

He sounded angry with her and Stephanie felt herself shiver.

'Tell me something,' he demanded bitterly. 'If the positions had been reversed, if you had been the one to die, do you honestly think that Paul would have lived the rest of his life as a monk?'

She made a small agonised sound at the back of her throat and instantly Gray leapt out of the bed, enfolding her in his arms, and rocking her against his hard frame, even though she struggled to break free of him.

The tears she hadn't been able to conceal poured from her eyes, soaking his shoulders.

He wasn't completely nude. He was wearing a brief pair of underpants, but he might as well have been, Stephanie reflected shakily, as she shivered in his arms.

Against her ear she could hear him crooning words of apology and comfort. There was nothing sexual in the way he was holding her; this was the Gray who had held and comforted her after Paul's death, the Gray she loved and respected as she did no other human being. But still lingering in the shadows was that other Gray ... the Gray who had looked at her with something approaching hate in his eyes when he opened them to see that she wasn't Carla. The Gray who had brutally made her aware of the fact that he was a man with all man's natural desires.

Now, gently, he held her away from him, using his knuckles to brush the tears from her face.

She felt herself shudder, and longed to be back in his arms, comforted by his bulk, protected by his caring. She felt cold and intensely alone, and yet, as she made a move towards him, he released her and stepped back, chiding her gently.

'I'm not made of stone, Steph.'

And he wanted a woman who was out of reach. She had learned the hard way from Paul, that the male sex could want and take women for whom they felt nothing emotionally.

'What's happening to us, Gray?' she asked him tearfully.

'Do you really need me to answer that?' He looked at her with brooding eyes. 'We're two people who know each other too well in some respects and not well enough in others. Come on, let's get some breakfast and then get out of here.'

Common sense urged her to tell him that she had changed her mind; that she wasn't going to go with him, but for some reason she said nothing. Why? Did she *want* to go back to the estuary with him?

Thoroughly confused, Stephanie set about making them both breakfast, while Gray went to have his shower.

The first thing Gray did when they arrived back in the village was to drop Stephanie outside his cottage, with the explanation that he wanted to go down to the yard to make sure nothing needed his attention.

Stephanie watched him go, her mouth drooping slightly with sadness and bewilderment. Gray had changed. Hitherto she had perceived him as being slightly remote, above the trials and tribulations that beset the rest of the human race, but now ...

But now she was being forced to confront the reality of his sexuality, she told herself unkindly, and she was jealous; jealous of Gray because he was able to experience those pleasures that were denied to her, and jealous of Carla because she was the woman who aroused the need for them within him.

Almost sick with self-disgust, she let herself into the

cottage and took the cases Gray had dropped off for her up to her room.

What was the matter with her? She was developing a selfish dog-in-the-manger attitude towards Gray that made her feel uncomfortably guilty about her own motives. Was she really so weak-minded that she resented Gray loving someone else?

Immediately her mind shied away from the question, her hands stilling for a moment as she tensed and stared unseeingly out of her bedroom window.

Gray had asked her for her help, and she had agreed to give it, but wasn't some part of her secretly pleased that Carla had given him up in favour of her husband?

Her mind fought in panic against the hardness of the accusation. She had been concerned for Gray, of course she had. Carla was a married woman. And if she hadn't been? A shudder of tension convulsed her body, a fine sheen of sweat dampening her skin. She was trembling violently, shivering so much that she had to wrap her arms round herself. Her thoughts were taking her along paths, raising spectres that she wasn't prepared to face.

The shrill sound of the telephone ringing was a welcome relief. She went downstairs to answer it. The caller identified himself as a 'Mac Weston', and asked for Gray.

She explained that he was down at the yard.

'Could you get him to give me a ring, as soon as possible? Tell him it's about the Fastnet. He knows my number.'

The Fastnet. Stephanie's hands were trembling when she replaced the receiver. Only the previous year bad weather had caused many of the entrants to withdraw from the race. Those who had persevered had battled against monstrous seas—several had capsized—some had lost their lives.

Her guilt over the failure of her marriage was somehow inextricably caught up in her fear of the sea. She shivered again, suddenly remembering the very last time she and Paul had gone out sailing together.

It had been after their relationship had started to deteriorate, not long before Paul's death. They had taken his boat out with the intention of sailing it to a small, uninhabited island off the coast. It had been Paul's idea; a way of making amends to her for their quarrel the evening before.

He had come in late—and drunk. He had hit her, she remembered, touching her cheek automatically, as though her flesh still bore the imprint of that blow.

They had set out early; she had packed a picnic. It was a perfect day for sailing, and Paul had been in high spirits. Almost like the old Paul; the Paul she had fallen in love with.

They had made good time to the island and had spent a couple of hours there, swimming and then having their lunch. It was mid-afternoon when they set off back. Paul's mood seemed to change immediately they got back on board.

The breeze had picked up and a stiff, fresh wind had been blowing, Stephanie remembered. Paul had sailed the small boat almost recklessly close to the wind, crowding on too much sail. When she cautioned him against it, he had lost his temper with her, delivering a furious tirade that had destroyed all her earlier pleasure in the day. Neither of them was wearing safety-jackets.

She had wanted to put hers on, but Paul had called impatiently that he was ready to leave, and now, as the small boat raced dangerously across the waves, she was beginning to regret the lack of this safety precaution.

She had called out to Paul to take in some of the sail, but he had ignored her, tacking so abruptly that she was flung to one side of the yacht as it keeled over. Instinctively she had clung to the side, closing her mouth against the incoming swell of sea water, waiting for the small craft to right itself, furious with Paul for putting them both in so much danger, and then . . .

It had been years since she had let herself remember this particular incident, and part of her didn't want to remember it now, Stephanie acknowledged, her body as cold as though it was still immersed in sea water. Even without closing her eyes, she could remember the scene in minute detail, feel the cold clamminess of her wet clothes, the numbness of her fingers, and the anger that had turned horrifyingly to fear as she realised that Paul was not going to help her; that he was deliberately trying to . . .

To what? she asked herself now. To drown her? Anxiously, she gnawed at her bottom lip. As she had learned after their marriage, Paul had an uncontrollable temper when aroused, but had he actually been trying to drown her that day, or had it simply been an accident . . . a misjudgement . . .?

While she was still clinging grimly to the side of the boat, a coastguard craft had come within hailing distance to them and, seeing her plight, had instantly come to her rescue.

Paul had explained away the mishap with his usual

charm, and although the coastguard had frowningly
pointed out that he was carrying far too much sail for
such a brisk wind, he had made no other comment.

Once they got home, Paul had been surly and
uncommunicative. He had left her there to go to
Southampton, she remembered, and she might have
thought no more about the incident, had it not been for
the fact that during a particularly vicious row some
days later, he had said, 'I want to be free of you,
Stephanie, and I will be—whatever I have to do to do it.'

Even now there were still occasions when she
dreamed about the incident, the cunning, almost
triumphant look in Paul's eyes as he watched her
struggles to maintain her grip on the boat. Had he
actually tried to drown her, or had it only been an
accident? She would never know.

Just as she would never know whether his death had
been an accident or . . . or a deliberate decision to escape
from her once and for all.

That haunted her, too; that she might have been
responsible for his death. It was like a sickness that she
carried round inside her; a poison that tainted her
whole life.

Jerking herself back to reality she pushed the bitter
memories away. She had to go down to the yard and
give Gray his message.

She saw the car first; a long, sleek Jaguar that looked
oddly out of place among the shabby boats and Gray's
rather battered Range Rover. She recognised it
immediately of course, a mixture of anger and pain
obliterating her earlier tension as she realised that Carla
was visiting the yard.

She saw them the moment she rounded the corner of the building, standing together, with barely an inch of space between them. Gray's dark head angled almost protectively over Carla's bent one. Her hand was on his arm, her finger-nails dark with polish. She was wearing a suede skirt with a toning silk blouse. Every blonde hair was in place.

As she watched, a small breeze sprang up and teased the smooth blonde bob. Gray reached out and tucked several silken strands behind her ear.

The ground beneath Stephanie's feet actually felt as though it moved as she watched the small, betraying tableau. Carla's hair looked like spun silver against the tanned masculinity of Gray's hand. She looked up at him, and although she couldn't hear what they were saying or see their expressions Stephanie had no doubt that she was watching an intimate moment between two lovers.

Off to her right a small movement caught her eye. She raised her head and then tensed as she saw Alex striding towards the other couple, still both oblivious to the fact that they were no longer alone.

Immediately Stephanie started to move, her one instinct to protect Gray.

She reached the engrossed couple several yards ahead of Alex, her hand reaching out to clutch Gray's arm, her eyes unknowingly dark with shock and fear.

'Stephanie. Is something wrong?'

Immediately Gray swung away from Carla, the hand that had so intimately touched her hair now covering the place where Stephanie's lay against his tanned forearm.

The sun was dazzling her, preventing her from seeing his expression, but she was aware of Carla stepping away from them to greet her husband, and her body tensed in dread, wondering if he had witnessed what she had seen and placed the same interpretation on it. If he had . . .

She forgot that the last thing on earth she wanted was for Gray to sail in the Fastnet, and immediately reached up on her toes, clutching at his shoulder to balance herself as she planted a kiss against his jaw and said huskily, 'No, nothing at all. I . . . I was just lonely without you . . .'

She could feel Gray's tension, and understood the reason for it, but by now he too was aware of Alex's presence, and as naturally as though they were indeed lovers he slid one arm round Stephanie's waist, curving her against his side, swinging her round so that the sunlight no longer dazzled her.

'Now that's what I like,' he responded in teasing tones. 'A woman who's not afraid to say she wants me.' The look in his eyes was that of an ardent lover, who could scarcely wait to be alone with his woman, and it threw her, confusing her, making her forget that she was still clinging to him like a fragile vine.

'I . . . I have a message for you . . .' She relayed it to him, stumbling over the words as she realised that his attention was focused on her mouth. The way he was looking at her was causing the most extraordinary sensations inside her. She realised of course that he was simply doing it for Alex's benefit; that it wasn't real.

The heat of his arm resting against her body seemed to burn right through her clothes. She could feel the imprint of his hard hip against her softer flesh, and where the side of her breast was pressed against his body a fiery ache was developing that was having the most devastating effect on her senses.

'I suspect that you and I are most definitely *de trop*, darling,' she heard Alex say laughingly to Carla.

'You two must come round and have dinner with us one night. What about next week? We should have the results of the sea trials in by then, shouldn't we, Gray?'

Without taking his eyes from her mouth, Stephanie heard Gray saying almost abstractedly, 'Yes . . . yes . . . I'm more than satisfied with her tests so far. I intend to take her out a couple more times—all I'm waiting for is a good gale.'

Numbly Stephanie stared up at him, her eyes going dark with shock and fear. She couldn't bear to think of losing Gray to the sea. She wanted to scream at him and beg him not to take such a risk. All her normally logical responses were swept away in the fierce tide of fear that burned through her.

Somewhere in the distance she was aware of car doors slamming and an engine starting, and that small part of her mind that was still functioning properly recognised that Carla and her husband must have left them; but all her concentration, all her attention was focused on Gray and the way he was still looking at her mouth.

A thrill of some dangerous and alien emotion raced through her. Without being aware of the provocation of what she was doing she touched her tongue-tip tentatively to the dry outline of her lips.

Someone shuddered. Herself, or Gray? She looked up at him, and trembled beneath the expression in his eyes.

'Do that again and I won't be responsible for what happens next,' he warned her in a curiously rusty, hoarse voice, that trapped her attention, focusing it on the shape of his mouth.

'For God's sake, Stephanie, do you *know* what you're doing? You're looking at me as though you can't wait to feel my mouth against yours.'

The words reached her, shocking her out of her momentary trance. She fought to break free of his enclosing arm, but instead of releasing her Gray pulled her hard against his body, his free hand sliding into her hair, trapping her so that she couldn't move.

She watched the downward descent of his head with a strange sensation of calm and disbelief.

His mouth touched hers, and she closed her eyes automatically. 'No ...' She felt the harsh objection against her mouth, and opened her eyes instinctively.

'I want to see what you're feeling when I kiss you.'

'Gray. No ... don't ...' She struggled to free herself, squirming against the almost painful hardness of his body, until she realised the effect her frantic movements were having on him.

He watched the hot colour scorch her skin with cynical detachment, demanding acidly, 'You're not that naïve, surely, Stephanie. Rub yourself against any normal man like that and you'd get exactly the same response.'

When her embarrassed colour deepened he smiled sardonically and bent his head to her ear and mouthed softly, 'I'm a man, Stephanie, and not a machine, and what you're doing to my body right now is driving me right out of my mind.'

His grip had slackened slightly and Stephanie pulled back, sickened and shaken by his bluntness. This wasn't the Gray she knew; the Gray who was always so courteous and careful of her, never allowing his masculinity to embarrass or disconcert her. This was another Gray, a Gray she was not familiar with. *Carla*'s Gray, she acknowledged achingly.

'What *I'm* doing to you?' she threw back at him bitterly. 'Don't you mean what seeing Carla has done to you? I'm not blind, Gray, I saw the way you were looking at her before. I saw how you touched her . . .'

Tears started up in her eyes, and she brushed them away impatiently, torn between misery and anger.

'I won't be used as a substitute for her, Gray. You told me it was all over between you. You . . .'

'It is,' he interrupted quietly, stepping back from her, his eyes watching her with cool dispassion.

'Alex saw the two of you together as well,' Stephanie told him uncertainly. 'That was why I . . .'

'Acted as though there was nothing you wanted more than my body against yours, my *mouth* against yours?' Gray derided savagely. 'Oh, you don't have to explain that to me, Stephanie. I know the score. For God's sake, you can't spend the rest of your life grieving over Paul.'

He was angry now, and she couldn't understand why, or how Paul had been dragged into the conversation. What did her relationship with Paul have to do with their present discussion?

She drew in a sharp breath, and remembered the way he had looked at Carla, with both tenderness and compassion, and she said bitterly, 'Why not? That's what you intend to do over Carla, isn't it?'

She saw him reach out towards her, but she moved back, turning on her heel and almost running out of the yard.

Once she was outside it, she slowed down to a more normal walk. Her chest felt tight and hurt, her eyes were smarting with unshed tears; her whole body was gripped with tension, and the turmoil of emotions inside her was something she had not experienced for years.

As she walked back to the cottage she tried to calm herself down a little. A group of fishermen stood by the harbour wall, chatting; one of them called out a greeting to her and she returned it.

How did the wives of these men cope? she wondered. Only last year there had been a terrible disaster, the entire crew of a trawler lost in heavy seas; some women had lost both husbands and sons. And yet she had heard one of them say on television that if her only surviving son should want to go to sea she would not try to stop him.

Where did such courage come from?

CHAPTER FIVE

STEPHANIE waited tensely for Gray's return, anticipating a confrontation following the way she had run out of the yard, but none was forthcoming.

Gray simply came into the kitchen where she was preparing their supper, and calmly started to help her as though nothing had happened.

It took her several seconds to realise that the feeling she was experiencing was something akin to disappointment, as she forced herself to follow his lead and respond to his casual conversation.

'With a bit of luck I'll be able to take the boat out tomorrow for more testing. They're forecasting heavy weather. Just what we need at this stage.'

She could almost feel herself blench as she listened to him, and he frowned, putting down the bowl of salad he had been preparing, and taking a gentle hold of her shoulders.

'Look, Steph, I understand how you feel about the sea, but it wasn't the sea that caused Paul's death, it was his own recklessness,' he told her bluntly. 'I'm sorry if that hurts you but it is the truth. Paul disregarded the safety precautions and that was why he drowned. You used to love sailing. I remember when your family first came to the estuary; you were never away from the yard.'

'Sailing was my father's hobby,' Stephanie told him

stupidly, as though they were strangers and he knew nothing about her.

'I know, and he taught you well. Too well for you to give it up completely. I used to see you handling that small dinghy of his. You were a pleasure to watch.'

Gray used to watch her. She stared at him. As a teenager he had seemed very remote and adult, a man while she and Paul were still little more than children. He had been kind to her though, she remembered that ... kind and patient ...

She remembered Paul teasing her once that Gray 'fancied' her ... How embarrassed she had been, and how she had resented Paul's teasing remark. How could a man like Gray ever want a girl of her age? She remembered now that Paul had often made similar remarks to her about his cousin; after they were married those remarks had taken on a gloating, unpleasant nuance she had instinctively shied away from.

The memory was a very selective thing; for instance, in the early days after Paul's death she had forgotten his cruelty, both mental and physical, and remembered only her adoration of him.

She had also forgotten how much Paul had seemed to resent Gray at times ... how much he had railed against his older cousin's influence with his parents.

Her parents had moved to the estuary when she was fifteen; she had been eighteen when she married Paul, and yet she had learned less about him in all those three years than she had in three months of marriage to him.

Paul had confessed to her once that Gray had been against their getting married. She had thought nothing of it at the time apart from being a little hurt that Gray, whom she looked upon as her friend, had chosen to align himself with their families.

'Come back . . .'

Gray's deep voice brought her back to the present, his eyes hardening slightly as he told her. 'I won't ask who or what you were thinking about, but whatever it was, it was obviously unpleasant. It's time you got over this phobia you have about the sea,' he added abruptly. 'What is it you fear so much? That you might drown?'

She shook her head forcefully, unable to explain to him that her fear was somehow linked with Paul's death, and those awful, terrifying moments alone in the yacht with him when she had thought he was going to let her drown. Ever since his death she had battled to keep those memories at bay, and she knew that to go sailing again would be to unlock the doors she had barred against them.

But weren't they already unlocked? Today, this afternoon, she had relived those traumatic moments and had found that, while the fear and panic remained, the dreadful soul-wrenching agony of fearing the man that she loved wanted to kill her had gone.

Not that she thought that Paul had deliberately and cold-bloodedly tried to drown her. It was just that she had seen in his face such a look of triumph and delight that she had sensed in him a wild desire to destroy her; that same desire she saw in him whenever he lost his temper with her and struck her. Paul had had an extremely volatile temperament, his emotions constantly see-sawing. Sometimes she had even wondered if he had perhaps been slightly unbalanced in some way. After all, he had been the one to persuade her into marriage, and he had been the one to grow tired of her once they were married, so quickly that in retrospect his feelings seemed to have changed overnight.

By mutual consent, she and Gray decided on an early night. She was tired, Stephanie admitted as she prepared for bed, but it wasn't a healthy tiredness, it was a mixture of strain and mental exhaustion.

What had happened to the Stephanie and Gray who used to stay up until all hours of the morning, talking animatedly to one another? It was as though Carla was proving to be a catalyst whose presence was causing her to dig deep into the past and re-evaluate very many things in her life. She was causing ripples on the surface of Stephanie's life that were nothing when compared with the deep and complex currents eddying dangerously, far below that surface.

Tomorrow she would start work at the yard, familiarising herself with its procedures, and thus freeing Gray to concentrate on testing his boat.

She fell asleep on that thought.

She was dreaming. She was sailing on an impossibly blue sea; and the bright sails of the small craft were silhouetted against an impossibly blue sky. It was warm, and there was a teasing, dancing breeze. She could see it billowing out the striped sails, filling them, sending the boat skimming across the water.

It was an exhilarating sensation, and automatically she lifted her face to the sun, her blood singing with pleasure and excitement.

She wasn't alone in the boat. There was a man with

her. He was controlling it. She felt safe and happy with him, free to enjoy the golden brilliance of the day and to give herself over to the thrill of matching her skills against those of the elements.

Sailing ... She had always loved it. She leaned forwards to tell Gray so, and he turned his head. Only he wasn't Gray, and she felt a scream of panic rise from her throat as she recognised Paul's face contorted in a grimace of hatred.

Suddenly both the sky and the sea turned black, and she was filled with fear.

She screamed out, and felt Paul lean towards her, taking hold of her.

'Stephanie ... Stephanie, wake up ...'

Shuddering, she opened her eyes. Gray was bending over her, his fingers biting into the soft flesh of her arms as he shook her.

He was wearing a robe and his hair was all tousled as though he had been woken abruptly from sleep.

'You were having a nightmare,' he told her curtly.

The lamp beside her bed had been switched on, its soft glow warming the dark room.

'You called out for Paul. You sounded terrified.'

She had been. She shuddered violently, remembering her dream. It had been so real ... so traumatic. Often in those first months after Paul's death she had dreamed, but in those dreams she had always been overwhelmed by guilt, and had always been reaching out to him, trying to save him.

It didn't take super-intelligence to understand why she had had this particular dream tonight though, but what she did find disturbing was her remembrance of how happy and safe she had felt when she had thought she was with Gray.

She sat up awkwardly, snatching at the sheet as it slipped away from her body. The nightdress she was wearing was a fine cotton lawn and, although she knew that Gray was hardly likely to be concerned about any momentary glimpse of her breasts, her gesture was the instinctive protective one of a woman not used to sharing intimacies with members of the opposite sex.

'I'm sorry if I disturbed you——' she began to apologise, but Gray cut her short, his mouth compressing, and twisting oddly as he interrupted sardonically, 'Are you?'

His reaction puzzled her, and she reached out automatically, her hand on his arm as he made to get up.

'Gray . . .'

'You're *never* going to get over him, are you, Stephanie? You're never going to let him go. You carry him about in your head with you . . . he shares your bed at night . . .' He broke off abruptly and said in a different voice, 'When you touched me this afternoon— were you pretending then that I was him?'

His accusation stunned her. Her eyes widened as she stared at him, pain forming a hard knot in her throat.

'No . . . no, of course I wasn't. I did that to protect you, to . . . Carla's husband had seen the two of you together. I . . .'

'You were only thinking of me, is that it? Well, perhaps it's time I repaid the favour, and reminded *you* exactly what it is you're turning your back on by clinging to your memories of a dead man.'

Before she could move, his hands were on her

shoulders, pushing her back against the pillows, his head descending so that it blotted out all the light.

She froze beneath the hard pressure of his mouth as it took hers in fierce determination. She could feel the sharp pressure of Gray's teeth against her lip and taste the rusty salt of her own blood. She made a muffled sound of protest and, as abruptly as he had taken hold of her, she felt him release her.

She was quivering with the shock of his unexpected attack. Never in a thousand wild imaginings had she ever believed that Gray would treat a woman like that. If she had given any thought to it at all she had supposed that he would be a considerate, caring lover, not . . .

Her fingers touched her swollen mouth, tears flooding her eyes.

'Stephanie, for God's sake, I'm sorry. I shouldn't have done that.'

Incredibly he was taking her back in his arms, and even more incredibly she was not resisting him. She felt the roughness of his robe beneath her cheek as he eased her against his shoulder. 'I . . .'

'I never thought you'd do a thing like that, Gray. I never thought you were the sort of man who . . . who liked . . . hurting women . . .'

Fresh tears brimmed from her eyes, and she heard him curse. It seemed incredible after what he had just done that she should have no fear of him. Perhaps her marriage to Paul had robbed her of the ability to experience any more sexual fear.

She heard Gray curse, and jerked back instinctively when his fingers slid along her jaw, cupping and tilting her face.

'Stephanie, I'm sorry. I'm sorry . . . I didn't mean to hurt you.' As he whispered the husky words of apology his lips moved caressingly against hers, imparting comfort and warmth. His arm tightened around her, and as his tongue started to trace the tender outline of her mouth she felt as though she were falling through space, helplessly spinning out of control; floating in a sea of sensations she could no longer understand.

Quite when her lips parted to the subtle persuasion of his tongue she didn't know.

It seemed as though one moment he was kissing her as though he was comforting a hurt child and the next the touch of his mouth had aroused such a storm of passion within her that she was clinging helplessly to him, responding to every passionate movement of his mouth against her own with a responsiveness that her conscious mind could only observe with awe and disbelief.

His robe had come open and her breasts were pressed against his chest, only the thin cotton of her nightdress between them.

His hands moulded her body, caressing her back, his touch making her spine arch, making her . . .

Abruptly she realised what she was doing, and in that same moment he released her, moving back from her. Both of them were breathing hard.

'*Were* you remembering Paul then, when I held you in my arms?' he demanded thickly. '*Were* you . . .?'

Shaken by the realisation of how much he had affected her, Stephanie cut across his raw demand with a shaky question of her own.

'Why not? After all, I know that *you* must have been thinking of Carla.' Her mouth twisted bitterly.

Gray got up abruptly and stood towering over her.

'Are you trying to tell me that you *were* pretending I was Paul?'

She didn't answer him. She couldn't. Not without lying, so instead she simply averted her head, and prayed for him to leave. She had experienced too much in far too short a space of time. Her emotions were in turmoil, her whole world had been turned upside-down and she needed to come to terms with what had just happened . . . with the fact that in Gray's arms she had responded to him in a way that she had never responded to any other man, and that included Paul.

When she had married Paul she had been little more than a child, in love with the idea of love. She had been happier exchanging kisses with him than she had making love, but just now in Gray's arms, for the first time in her life she had experienced the reality of physical arousal and need.

She had wanted Gray to go on touching and kissing her. She had wanted . . . She drew a shuddering breath, and her senses relayed to her the fact that he was moving away.

He opened the door and she turned her head to look at him, praying that he wouldn't read what was in her eyes.

'I'll leave you to your dreams of Paul, then,' he told her harshly. 'It seems that you get more satisfaction from them than you do from reality.'

She wanted to cry out to him, to stop him and tell him the truth, but what was the point? He loved Carla.

And she loved him!

It hit her like a sledge-hammer blow, knocking her

whole world out of focus, while she grappled with the enormity of it.

Of course she loved him, she tried to reason with herself, but as a sister . . . as a friend . . . but her body and her heart mocked her for her cowardice; they wanted him as a man . . . as a lover.

'Oh, God!' She wasn't sure if she said the words out loud or not. What on earth was she going to do? The sensible thing would be to pack her bags and leave first thing in the morning, but how could she do that? She had given Gray her promise to help him, and if she hadn't realised it already, his out-of-character behaviour tonight must have shown her just how much he was suffering.

Loving Carla was tearing him apart. So much so that he had been tempted to vent his physical frustration with her, Stephanie.

The pain that followed that admission was appallingly enlightening. It was a shock to a woman who considered herself to be lacking in sexuality to discover how wantonly her body was reacting to the thought of Gray as her lover.

But he wouldn't have been *her* lover, she reminded herself bitterly, he would have been Carla's and she would have been her substitute.

They were friends, and she would have to content herself with that. Maybe one day . . .

Maybe never, she told herself hardily. She would be a fool if she spent the rest of her life longing for a man who could never be hers. Gray loved Carla, he had told her so.

It took her a long time to get to sleep. Perhaps it was

only her emotionally heightened senses, she didn't know, but the scent of him seemed to cling to her skin, disturbing her, making her ache and yearn for things that could never be.

At last she drifted off to sleep but, although she longed to do so, she did not dream of Gray.

During the night the weather changed. Stephanie heard the wind the moment she woke up. For several minutes she simply lay drowsily listening to it. It was a comforting, noisy sound—when one was tucked up warmly in bed.

Through her open window she could smell salt, and deep down inside she felt a flicker of long-forgotten excitement. She and her father had spent many blustery days out in the Channel, before Paul's death and her own guilt had crippled her with fear.

Gray had been right about the weather, and now he would be able to undertake sea trials on his boat.

Gray! Instantly she sat up in bed, colouring hotly as she remembered how he had kissed her last night and how she had responded.

He had been trying to make her forget Paul, but he didn't know the truth about Paul or their marriage. He thought she was still deeply in love with his cousin.

Even before she went downstairs, some new sixth sense she had developed overnight told her that Gray had gone out. She found a note propped up against the kettle, informing her that he had left early and would be spending the day testing the boat.

The house felt empty without him and she felt restless. The phone rang just as she was setting out, and the shock of hearing Carla's voice on the other end of the line made her freeze with pain.

'Gray isn't here,' she managed ungraciously when she eventually found her voice.

'I was ringing to arrange that dinner date.'

Carla was ignoring her comment and Stephanie realised that the other woman might not be alone, and that her husband might be able to hear her conversation. Or was the dinner party simply an excuse she was using because Gray wasn't there?

'What about next Wednesday? Are you both free that evening?'

Making small talk with the woman that Gray loved was like trying to speak after her throat had been rubbed raw with sandpaper, but since Gray had made no objection to the invitation, she felt she had to go along with it, and confirm the arrangement.

Part of her longed to demand that Carla leave him alone, to ask her if she knew what the game she was playing with him was doing to him, but she knew that Gray would not thank her for her interference.

How could he love a woman like that? A woman who saw him only as a diversion from her marriage. A woman who frankly admitted that she preferred to stay with her wealthy husband. Had Carla no feelings, no compassion? She couldn't love Gray. If she did ...

It was several minutes after the phone call had ended before Stephanie was able to bring herself to set out for the yard. She had dressed sensibly, in comfortable faded jeans, a cotton shirt and a warm jumper.

The wind buffeted her the moment she stepped outside, rain-clouds racing across the sky, driven by its surging gusts. Beyond the estuary the sea looked choppy, with white-capped waves further out to sea.

She had intended to listen to the shipping forecast before leaving the house but Carla's telephone call had driven it from her mind.

The men working in the yard called out a greeting to her as she walked past and let herself into the office. The phone was ringing as she walked in, and it seemed to go on ringing all morning, so that it was almost lunchtime before she had time to switch on the portable radio she had found on the muddled desk.

She was just in time to catch the last of the gale warnings, and her stomach heaved with nervous anxiety as she heard the newsreader announcing a gale and heavy seas off the Channel.

Gray would have taken the boat out into the open sea, she knew that. How would he be able to test its rough weather endurance without doing so? She knew enough about sailing to understand the reason behind his early-morning start.

She heard a car outside and glanced out of the window, her heart dropping as she recognised Alex's Jaguar.

Resentment stabbed through her. What did Carla want? Hadn't she hurt Gray enough already?

Only it wasn't Carla who got out of the car, it was Alex himself. He strode towards the office and she went to let him in.

'The weather's worsening,' he commented as he came in.

'Yes, I've just heard the shipping forecast.'

He was a good-looking man, she acknowledged, with an air of calm dependability.

'Try not to worry, Gray knows what he's doing. I've got one hell of a lot of money tied up in that boat he's out in, and you don't think I'd let him handle it if I didn't have absolute faith in him, do you?'

Her eyes widened as she read the message in his eyes. He *knew* that she was frightened. How? Had Gray told him about her hang-up about the sea?

She frowned. She wouldn't have thought that he and Gray would be that close—not with them both loving the same woman.

Her private knowledge about Gray's love for Carla made her feel acutely uncomfortable with Alex. He seemed such a pleasant man; a strong man too, not one she would have thought who would be drawn to a woman as faithless as Carla.

'I've a radio at home, Gray's just called in to say he's on his way back. I thought you'd like to know. He should be back about seven,' he added, glancing at his watch.

Stephanie cleared her throat. She was stunned that Alex had taken the time to come down here and reassure her about Gray's safety, and then she remembered that as far as Alex was concerned, she and Gray were lovers.

'I . . . thanks for letting me know,' she said lamely, adding awkwardly, 'Is Gray pleased with today's tests?'

She hardly knew what to say. She felt uncomfortable and ill at ease with Alex, even while she appreciated his kindness. She hated feeling that she was in any way a party to Carla's deception of him, and she wondered bitterly how on earth Gray managed to work alongside him. Perhaps his own love for Carla freed him from any normal feelings of guilt.

'Very,' Alex responded, apparently unaware of her constraint. 'We're using a revolutionary new keel—something along the lines the Australians used for the America's Cup—but I expect Gray's told you all about that. It's his design—it gives the boat greater speed and manoeuvrability. With a little bit more research and development, it could be modified for use with smaller, more commercial craft, but of course you know all about his plans for the development of the yard. It's fortunate that your own career is such that you can work almost anywhere. Carla gave up hers after our first child was born and I felt very guilty about it. She'd always loved her work.'

Carla working? Stephanie tried to visualise what line of work the glamorous blonde had been in. Modelling seemed the most likely choice.

'What exactly did she do?' she asked, unable to restrain her curiosity.

'She's a psychiatrist. She worked mainly with adolescents. It was very demanding, but I know she misses it.'

Stephanie looked at him in stunned disbelief. A psychiatrist! So Carla had brains as well as beauty. Brains, beauty, but no heart, she reflected acidly.

'I'd better be on my way, but I promised Gray I'd come down and give you the good news.'

She watched him walk to his car through a blur of angry tears. Gray's concern hadn't been for her; he had simply wanted to make sure that Alex didn't suspect anything.

His behaviour was so at odds with the Gray she had

thought she knew, and yet she couldn't despise him for it, even though she knew that she would have condemned his behaviour in any other man.

Had she ever known him at all? Had she ever known herself? she wondered bitterly. After all, she hadn't known that she loved him until last night.

She moved, restless, wanting to forget the physical sensations he had aroused in her the previous night. She wanted to forget the sensation of his mouth possessing her own, his hands . . . With a taut sound of anger, she spun round on her heel and started to attack the large pile of filing stuffed into one of the metal trays.

By mid-afternoon it was raining, and her nerves were stretched to breaking-point as she looked out at the angry sea. There were no small sails out in the estuary now, and Bob, the oldest and most experienced of the boat-yard's employees, an ex-trawlerman who had lost a leg in a fishing accident, prophesied that it would get worse before it got better.

At five o'clock the men went home. She had done all the filing, the post was up to date, and she was sick of prowling restlessly round the confining office. She might as well go back to the cottage.

It was only a matter of a hundred yards or so walk, but she was glad of the heavy-duty jacket she had taken from the laundry room on her way out, as she tugged the collar up against the sheeting rain.

The jacket belonged to Gray, and whether it was the dampness in the air or her own imagination, she didn't know, but it seemed as though the scent of his body clung tantalisingly to the heavy wool.

When he came in he would be tired, cold and hungry,

and because it was easier to busy herself with practical things than to sit anxiously counting the minutes until his return, she went upstairs to check that there were plenty of fresh towels in the bathroom and that the water was hot.

The woman who normally took care of the house was on holiday, but Stephanie had enough experience of sailing herself to know exactly what Gray would want to eat once he got back—something fast and hot.

She opted for chilli, knowing that it wouldn't spoil if he got back later than expected.

At half-past six, a whole half-hour before Gray's earliest time of arrival, she was tense with nervous anxiety. Over and over in her mind, like a video played in slow motion, she saw him being swept overboard, destroyed by the seas as Paul had been. She told herself that Gray was a far better sailor than Paul had ever been, that he had more experience, more caution, that he was perfectly safe—but none of it mattered.

If this was what she was like when he was simply out testing the new boat, what would she be like when he actually took part in the Fastnet?

She shuddered visibly, chafing her goose-pimpled arms with tense hands. Despite the fact that the central heating was on, she was cold.

On impulse she went outside, the strength of the wind whipping back her hair and making her catch her breath. There was a store of dry logs kept just outside the laundry room and she filled a basket with them.

Lighting a fire would keep her hands occupied, even if it did nothing to relieve the tension of her mind.

The crackle of the logs as the dry tinder caught fire

betrayed how tensely silent the room had been. She sat in front of the flames, staring unseeingly into them, Gray's face dancing in the yellow glare.

A door slammed and she stiffened, remembering that she had come in without locking the back door. She had lived in London for long enough to be aware of the danger of unwanted intruders.

She stood up, every nerve-ending alive with tension. The sitting-room door opened and her tension evaporated in a sob of relief as she saw Gray framed there.

He was still wearing his oilskins, the hood of his jacket pushed back to reveal the wet unruliness of his hair.

For a moment she was too choked with emotion to speak. He was back. He was safe. She wanted to run to him and be caught up in his arms. She wanted . . . She swallowed, feeling the tension within her increase.

'A fire—great. I'm frozen.'

Unlike her, Gray was completely relaxed.

'You . . . you're back early. Alex told me seven or later.'

'Yes, I asked him to. I knew if I was more than five minutes late you'd be worrying yourself silly.'

For no reason at all tears filled her eyes. Gray saw them.

In three strides he was at her side, filling the air around her with the clean, salty scent of the sea and cold, fresh air. She could smell the wind and the rain on his clothes and she wanted to reach out and touch him.

'There's nothing to cry about.'

He reached for her and would have wrapped her in his arms if she hadn't stepped away. Stephanie saw him frown and gnawed miserably at her bottom lip.

'You're all wet,' she complained huskily. 'There's plenty of hot water, and I've made a chilli.'

She was gabbling idiotically, she knew, but she couldn't stop herself. It was her only defence against flinging herself into his arms and confessing to him just how she felt.

Before, she had longed to experience love, to feel what other women felt, but now she wished whole-heartedly that she could return to her earlier companionable friendship with Gray. Loving him and knowing that he could never love her put a strain on her nervous system she wasn't sure it was able to bear.

CHAPTER SIX

AFTER supper, Gray rang Alex and spent some time on the telephone telling him how pleased he had been by the yacht's performance.

Supper had been a quiet meal. Gray had eaten his chilli hungrily, with the appetite of a man who had been out in the open air all day, but Stephanie had only been able to nibble at hers.

Her appetite seemed to have deserted her completely. She was tired as well. Not the healthy tiredness that came from enjoyable physical activity, but the draining, exhausting lassitude that followed intense emotional trauma.

One of her favourite hobbies was tapestry work. She used her own designs, which appealed to the artistic side of her nature, while the practical work of stitching the designs was very soothing.

A London friend had commissioned from her a set of six chair-seats for her rambling Cotswold cottage, and she was half-way through the work. Each seat-cover depicted a scene that had some relevance in her friend's life, and while Gray was on the telephone she went upstairs to collect her work. It took her longer than usual to become engrossed in what she was doing, at least half of her concentration unashamedly focused on Gray's conversation.

When he eventually hung up he was smiling

contentedly as he walked over to join her.

'You're pleased with your progress so far then?' she asked him as he sat down opposite her and picked up a book from the coffee table.

'Yes, very.'

Her heart sank. Only now was she prepared to admit to herself that she had hoped that somehow the yacht would not pass muster and he would change his mind about the Fastnet.

The silence wrapped round them as Stephanie worked on her tapestry, and Gray read his book. It should have been a companionable silence, but it wasn't.

Stephanie was acutely conscious of every movement he made; every time he turned a page she looked up; every time the fire crackled and spat she used it as an excuse to study him.

At last she couldn't stand it any longer. Putting aside her work, she got up.

'I'll go and make us some coffee.'

'No, you sit down, I'll do that. You made the supper, it's my turn now,' Gray told her easily, putting down his book and pushing her gently back into her chair.

The moment she felt his fingertips touch her arm, she flinched. She couldn't help it. The shock of him touching her, when she had yearned so much for some contact between them, had her cowering back in her chair petrified that she might betray herself in some way and that he would see how she felt about him.

Immediately, his expression changed, his smile turning to grim surveillance of her tense features. His hands locked round her upper arms, causing her to tense even more.

'What's the *matter* with you?' he demanded bitterly. 'I'm not going to hurt you, Steph.'

But he already was, and although he didn't know it, his words were an exact echo of the ones Paul had used to her so often after he had lost his temper with her and was trying to coax her round.

Immediately, it was as though she were back in the past, and it was Paul who was holding her so tightly, Paul who was looking down at her. Paul . . .

She gave a small moan of panic, and cried out hoarsely, 'No, no, please don't hurt me . . .'

Immediately his hands dropped away, his face registering his shock. 'Hurt you? For God's sake, Steph, I *wouldn't* hurt you.'

He sounded so tortured that her fear dropped away, leaving in its place a need to comfort and reassure him.

'No . . . not you . . . I . . . for a moment, I thought you were Paul.' The husky words seemed to hang on the air while they stared at one another. It seemed to Stephanie that they were seeing each other properly for the first time.

'*Paul* used to hurt you?' Gray demanded incredulously.

Too late, Stephanie realised the trap she had set for herself. She moistened her lips with the tip of her tongue, her throat dry with nervousness.

'Stephanie?'

'No . . . no . . . I . . .'

Her denial was so obviously a lie that she didn't blame Gray for the hard look that tautened his face.

'You're lying to me,' he gritted. 'I want the truth, and I intend to have it—no matter how long it takes. For ten years you've been acting like a tragedy queen, who's lost everything that made life worth living, and now you tell me . . .' He shook his head and she caught the bleak bafflement in his eyes before he lowered his gaze.

'I always knew that Paul had a wild streak—he could be violent as a child, but I never imagined . . . He did hurt you, didn't he?' he demanded thickly. 'And yet despite that you loved him. You all but fell apart when he was drowned.'

'No . . . no, I didn't love him,' Stephanie heard herself whispering, her own shock as great as Gray's, as his eyes mirrored the stunned expression in hers.

'I fell apart because of my guilt. Can't you understand, Gray? He had already told me how much he hated being married to me. He wanted to be free.' She moistened her lips again, not seeing the man standing in front of her, her thoughts back in the past. 'When he got angry . . . his tempers . . .' She shook her head in despair. 'I thought he might have deliberately let himself drown to escape from me.'

She heard Gray make a bitter, derisive sound in his throat and her eyes lifted to his in tragic entreaty.

'Not Paul,' he told her roughly. 'He loved life and himself far too much for that. Don't blame yourself for his accident, Stephanie, you mustn't do that. I know he had a bad temper, and probably said . . . unkind things, but he did love you.'

'No.' She marvelled that she could say it so calmly, 'No, Gray, he *didn't* love me,' she repeated quietly. 'He wanted me, and the only way he could have me was through marriage. I was so naïve, I didn't really understand. I thought he did love me, but he soon grew tired of my inexperience, of my——' She flushed deeply and forced herself to look directly at him. '—my lack of sexuality.'

She could feel the tension surrounding them and realised that it wasn't coming from her, but from Gray. He was looking at her as though he was on the point of erupting into blazing anger, and for a second she automatically flinched.

He reached out and touched her arm, keeping his eyes on her face. 'I promise you you have nothing to fear from me, Stephanie. Do you believe that?'

His voice was deep, and reassuring; she felt as though she could drown in the intensity of his eyes. A flood of relief and warmth swelled up inside her, and she smiled shakily at him.

'Paul used to say that I wasn't really a woman, that sexually I was still a child. I . . . I bored him. I . . . I didn't like it when we made love. He had someone else, I think, in Southampton. He used to go there a lot.'

Suddenly she wanted to tell him everything; she wanted to unburden herself of the secrets she had kept for so long. But most of all she wanted to look into his face and see there the knowledge that he refuted Paul's accusations; that in Gray's eyes, she *was* a woman . . . that she *was* desirable.

That knowledge brought her to an abrupt halt, hot colour flooding her skin, until it burned with painful intensity. Immediately, her lashes dropped, concealing her expression from him, in case he read what she was thinking. What was happening to her? What could she possibly gain from manoeuvring Gray into telling her she was a desirable woman?

If he had desired her she would have known it before now; he would have betrayed it to her without the need for any words.

A feeling of desolation swept over her, making her droop slightly in unconscious defeat.

'And despite all that you went on loving him ... mourning him.'

She couldn't look at Gray. It was enough to hear the condemnation in his voice.

She shook her head, her voice husky and unsteady.

'No ... I realised very quickly that what I loved was the idea of being in love. I had been playing at being an adult. Once Paul realised how ... how disappointing I was in bed he soon destroyed all my illusions. He told me he had only married me because it was the only way he could get me into bed.' She drew a shaky breath. 'I think we'd been married less than a month when I realised what I'd done.'

She heard Gray swear, but she couldn't look at him. She felt too ashamed. This was his cousin she was talking about. He must hate her for saying these things about Paul.

'You *knew* that, but you stayed with him?' His fingers dug into her arms as he grabbed hold of her and swung her round to the light. 'Why ... why, Stephanie? Did your parents know what he was doing to you?'

She shook her head, her throat choked with tears. 'I couldn't tell them. Don't you *see*, Gray?' she cried desperately, reading the grim lack of comprehension in the hard line of his mouth. 'It was *my* fault . . . *mine* . . . If I'd been better in bed . . . more responsive . . . less frigid.' She shuddered as she dragged out the word.

Instantly Gray released her, turning his back towards her, and she sensed that he did not want her to see his expression.

Her whole body went rigid. It was just as she had thought. He *was* angry with her, he was blaming her for Paul's death.

'*Why* haven't you ever told me any of this before? *Why* did you let me think you loved him . . . that you mourned him?'

He delivered the questions in rapid succession, in an even, careful tone, as though he was frightened of doing something violent.

Her throat went dry. 'I . . .'

Suddenly he spun round, catching her off guard as he grabbed hold of her. His eyes were blazing with emotion, his muscles straining under the control he was exercising over his body.

His anger swamped her fear and sparked off an answering response within her, freeing her from the thrall of her guilt.

Firelight illuminated both their faces as they stood opposite one another—like adversaries, Stephanie thought achingly.

'Because I *couldn't* . . . I couldn't tell anyone.' She saw his eyes harden, and continued bitterly, 'You can't imagine what it was like. Knowing that I was a failure as a woman . . . knowing that my lack of response frustrated Paul so much that it made him violent. And people wonder why there have been no other men in my life,' she added wildly. 'Well, now you know . . .'

'Because you're frightened that another man would hurt you—use violence against you?'

She shook her head despairingly. Had what she just said made so little impact on him!

'No, not that. Paul only hit me because I failed him as a woman. I told you, Gray, there's something wrong with me. I . . .' She avoided looking at him and swallowed thickly. 'I don't like sex.'

There was a long, tense silence that sawed at her fragile nerves, and eventually she risked looking at him. He was staring into the fire, his face averted from hers.

When at last he spoke, his words caused a shock that thundered through her.

'Have you ever thought that Paul might have been the one at fault? That he might have been responsible for your inability to respond to him? Have you ever tried to find out if any other man affects you in the same way? Have you never even *tried* to love someone else, Stephanie?'

The words hit her like blows. She opened her mouth to deny them and then closed it again, her eyes widening as she took in their full, shocking impact.

Of course she loved someone else. She loved *him*, but how could she tell him that? Gray had enough problems of his own without taking on the burden of hers, and she knew him well enough to know that he would try to do so.

'I . . .' She shook her head. 'I . . . no . . .'

A strange expression crossed his face as she voiced

the lie; one she found it impossible to read.

'Paul couldn't have been the one at fault,' she went on quietly. 'I . . . I know there were other girls, both before and after we were married.'

'I'm sure there were,' Gray conceded grimly. 'But knowing my hot-headed, selfish cousin, if he gave them any more pleasure than he gave you I should be extremely surprised.'

'You're . . . you're not angry with me, then?'

She had to ask the question, had to know if he still accepted her.

'Angry?' He frowned and looked at her as though the meaning of the words was unfamiliar to him.

'Paul was your cousin,' she elucidated. 'You . . . I . . .'

'For God's sake!' Suddenly he seemed furious. 'And because of that, you expect me to condone what he did to you? I thought you knew me better than that, Stephanie,' he said bitterly. 'I am angry, yes, but not with you. Paul always was a selfish little b . . .' He broke off, quite obviously fighting for control. 'It's just as well for his sake that he isn't alive. Because if he was . . . I'm not a violent man, but when I think of what he's done to you . . .'

He swore briefly, shocking her, his face contorted with rage and pain.

Slowly, like dawn creeping in on a winter morning, gladness was replacing the fear in her heart. Gray *hadn't* rejected her! He still cared about her. He was still her friend. She started to tremble, slow tears gathering in her eyes and rolling down her face.

She heard Gray make a muffled sound deep in his

throat and then she was in his arms, her face pressed against his neck.

'What is it? What did I say?'

'Nothing. I'm just so happy that you're still my friend.'

She felt his whole body tense as he held her away from him. 'Your *friend*?'

There was an odd note in his voice, a combination of acceptance and almost bitterness. 'Does my friendship mean that much to you then, Stephanie?'

'Everything,' she assured him truthfully. 'Much, much more than I can ever put into words.'

It was only later that she realised she might as well have been making a declaration of love, but, at the moment the words were uttered, all she was conscious of was the tenderness of Gray's smile and the warmth in his eyes as they stood together in front of the fire.

'How does all this fit in with your phobia about the sea?' he asked her some minutes later.

His question stunned her. She had opened her heart to him and told him so much, but there were still some things she could not bring herself to voice. Panic flared briefly in her eyes, and she shook her head.

'I . . . I don't know.'

She suspected he guessed that she was lying, but he didn't press her. It was only later when they were both on their way to bed that he referred to their conversation again. She was walking towards the door when he stopped her, saying softly, 'You know, Steph, there's a school of thought that says there are no frigid women, only inept men. Next time you get an attack of guilt over Paul, I should try thinking about that if I were you.'

She smiled shakily at him from the doorway. She had reached the door, but his words stopped her. Before she could stop herself she heard herself saying huskily, 'It's just as well you're in love with Carla, Gray, otherwise I might . . .' Appalled by her own stupidity, she broke off in mid-sentence.

'Might what? Want me to prove that statement with actions and not words?'

Hot colour spread betrayingly over her skin at his quick grasp of her thoughts.

'Would you like me as your lover, Steph?'

The words seemed to hang on the air, tormenting her. What would he say if she told him? She swallowed hard, and wondered if he knew how weak and shaky she felt. It was her own fault; she should never have uttered what had, after all, been an openly provocative remark.

'I . . . I . . .' She was looking everywhere but at him, but even so she was still aware of him coming towards her.

'We're just friends, Gray. You love Carla!' she managed to blurt out just before he reached her, instantly turning on her heel and almost running upstairs.

In her room she sank down on to the bed, her hands cupping her hot face. Dear God, what had come over her? She had practically begged Gray to make love to her. Had she no pride? No self-respect?

She was deeply asleep when Gray's hand on her shoulder shook her awake. It was just barely light and she stared groggily up at him. He was dressed in jeans and a fine cotton shirt. Alarm spread through her as she realised how early it was, a sudden spiral of fear replacing her initial embarrassment as the events of the evening came rushing back.

'What's wrong?'

'I need you down at the yard.'

He looked so grim that she didn't even think of asking what for, but simply dived out of bed, showering and dressing quickly, the moment he left her room.

In the kitchen he had coffee and toast ready for her, barely giving her time to eat and drink before bustling her outside. No one else was about; it was too early. The tide was just on the turn, and the sea lay still and calm under the lightening sky. During the night the storm had died, and already the sky was flushed with the promise of a fine day.

Gray was walking so fast it was hard work keeping up with him; she was too breathless to question him when they reached the yard, and instead of heading for the office he swung off in the direction of the deep-water moorings.

The yacht he was using for the Fastnet lay at anchor. Stephanie caught her breath as she glimpsed the beautiful craft. Fear mingled with admiration for her sleek lines.

Gray was walking on to the wooden pier, expecting her to follow him. She hesitated momentarily and then went after him. He stopped alongside the yacht and turned to wait for her. What was so important that he had rushed her down here almost before it was light?

She saw that he was frowning and felt a familiar tug of anxiety. 'Gray, what's wrong?' she demanded as she caught up with him.

'That's what I'm just about to find out.'

She was taken off guard when he bent down and picked her up in his arms. When she realised he was carrying her on board the yacht she cried out in protest, struggling to break free, but his grip on her body only tightened.

Like all racing yachts, its cabin was strictly functional and full of equipment. A life-jacket lay on one of the two bunks and as he put her down, Gray said, shockingly, 'I think that should be your size, put it on.'

And then, before she could object, he turned his back on her, leaving her to hammer helplessly on the closed door as he stepped outside and locked it against her.

Panic and anger kept her hammering on the door long after she realised that he wasn't going to let her out. She heard the engine start, and felt the movement of the yacht as it left its mooring.

Gray was taking her out to sea! Sheer surprise held her motionless as she realised what was happening. He must have planned to do this . . . getting her up when it was too early for anyone else to see them . . . providing her with a life-jacket. And then she remembered his cryptic words as he carried her on board. He was doing this because he thought it would reveal why she was so terrified of sailing.

With that came the realisation that he was not going to allow her to go ashore until he decided that she could. There was no point in her hammering on the door any longer. She had already bruised her knuckles and broken the skin.

Full of self-pity and misery, she sank down on to the hard bunk, automatically pulling on the life-jacket. Old habits died hard, and her father had taught her to be cautious and safety-conscious.

The jacket wasn't a new one. It smelled elusively of perfume, a perfume she had smelled before, Carla's perfume, she recognised, with a renewed spurt of rage.

Had Gray and Carla made love here on the yacht? She looked round at the cramped quarters and grimaced to herself. Hardly. It was amazing what fantasies the jealous mind could conjure up, and yet she knew that if Gray came to her now and said he loved her, she wouldn't care what their surroundings were.

But that was the difference between herself and Carla. She loved Gray, and she was convinced that the other woman did not.

They were well out into the Channel before Gray put the yacht on automatic and came down and unlocked the door. They stared at one another in silence.

'I thought you were my friend,' Stephanie said almost childishly at last.

His face grim, Gray replied, 'I am. Why else would I be doing this? There's something you're not telling me, Stephanie. Something that's festering inside you like poison.'

'And you think kidnapping me and bringing me on your yacht will release it, is that it?' she demanded angrily.

'You used to love sailing,' Gray responded obliquely.

'I remember that as a teenager you used to have such an intense love of life. Paul destroyed that.'

'And you think by bringing me out here you can restore it?'

'I don't know,' he said quietly. 'You tell me, can I?'

She didn't answer him. How could she? How could she tell him that her morbid fear of the sea was a two-pronged thing. She didn't just have Paul's death to contend with, she had her own far-too-vivid memories of icy sea water closing over her head, of numb fingers slowly loosing their grip on a slippery surface; of a man's face contorted into a mask of bitter determination as he watched her slowly lose her grip on life.

'Why don't you come up on deck and help me sail this lady?'

She didn't want to, but to stay down here alone with her memories and fears would be even worse. Numbly she followed him, hating him almost as much as she loved him.

She had never been on such a sophisticatedly equipped craft and she froze to an abrupt halt when Gray called out sharply to her, wondering what on earth she had done wrong.

'Safety lines,' he told her when she looked at him. 'Come over here and I'll fix it on for you.'

A safety line. She stared at the nylon rope and then back at Gray, feeling as though an enormous weight had suddenly been lifted from her shoulders.

With a safety line she couldn't slide overboard and be drowned. She would be safe! Trembling with relief, she let Gray clip on the sturdy harness, immediately awash with a feeling of gratitude.

'Feeling better now?' Gray asked her when he was sure the harness was secure.

'Yes . . . Yes.' She smiled shakily at him. 'I feel much better.' Her fear of the water receded and she lifted her face into the breeze, breathing in lungfuls of the clean, salty air.

Suddenly she felt exhilaratingly alive. More alive than she had felt in years. She wanted to laugh and cry at the same time. She felt free, she realised. Free of Paul, free of the past, and most of all, free of fear.

CHAPTER SEVEN

THE HOURS that followed had an almost magical quality about them. It was as though by some special power Gray had transported her back to the past, to a time before she had experienced reality and pain.

He was an expert sailor, taking no unnecessary risks even in such placid seas as they had today. Her fear gone, Stephanie was free to enjoy again something that had always given her special pleasure.

At lunchtime Gray dropped anchor and hauled out a watertight picnic box.

'You planned all this deliberately, didn't you?' Stephanie accused, watching him unpack foil-wrapped chicken, and garlic-flavoured bread to put in the small oven. There was fruit, cheese and fresh salad, too, and her mouth watered, her appetite sharpened by the sea air.

'Yes,' Gray admitted without hesitation. 'After what you told me about Paul it struck me that your fear of the sea might not have sprung quite so much from his death as from a desire to punish yourself for it.' He held up a hand to stop her when she would have interrupted him.

'I know it's the easiest thing in the world to play amateur psychiatrist, but hear me out, Steph. You loved sailing. When Paul was drowned, ending the fiasco that your marriage had become, it was like a prison door opening for you, but like anyone else in the same circumstances you felt guilty—more so perhaps because

Paul had already taught you to feel guilty—to shoulder the blame for the problems in your relationship. And because you felt guilty you had to punish yourself, just as Paul used to punish you, so you took away from yourself one of the things you enjoyed the most . . .'

He watched as she plucked tensely at the wool of the blanket he had put down on the hard bunk. She wasn't looking at him, and he wished desperately that she would so that he could see her reaction. Was she strong enough to take what he had just thrown at her? Or . . . or was the damage Paul had done to her so severe that . . .?

He got up abruptly, unable to endure thinking about his cousin. It was just as well he was dead. When he thought of what Paul had done to Stephanie, of how he had destroyed her as a woman and left her with a legacy of pain and fear . . .

'Stephanie, look at me. I don't want to hurt you—in any way.' The raw urgency in his voice made her lift her head. His eyes were brilliant with compassion and concern, and she felt the shock of what he had said to her recede, leaving in its place a warmth that seemed to spread throughout her body.

Gray cared. Perhaps he didn't love her in the way she loved him, but he still cared enough to want to break down the barriers imprisoning her. Enough to believe what she had told him without question. Perhaps enough to . . .

To what? Free her from her repressions by making love to her?

The thought whispered seductively through her mind, almost paralysing her with shock. She couldn't speak or move. *Gray* make love to her? She shivered, unaware that his eyes darkened with strain and fear for her.

How long had the desire for Gray to make love to her lain dormant in her subconscious? She shivered again, suddenly and quite illogically remembering the spring before Paul had started to pursue her in earnest.

She and her father had been sailing. Gray had been there when they came back. He had helped her off her father's small craft, lifting her bodily out of the boat. The memory of how he had held her—the sun on her back, the smell of salt and fresh air, the flurry of excitement beating through her veins—came back to her in startling detail.

That had been the moment she first became aware of Gray as a man and herself as a woman. She had haunted the yard for days after that, but Paul had been there and not Gray. And then Paul had started pursuing her and . . . and she had forgotten until now that all those years ago she had looked at Gray and wanted him.

'Stephanie, what's wrong?'

She blinked and was back in the present, suddenly aware of the rough urgency in Gray's voice. Her eyes focused on his face, surprised to see how strained he looked.

The smile she gave him was brief, her eyes still clouded with memories.

Paul, he thought savagely, hating his dead cousin. She had been thinking about Paul.

After that the day seemed to change; the sparkle dying out of it. It seemed to Stephanie that Gray was suddenly preoccupied and distant, and she wondered if he was wishing that Carla was with him.

Had she been, they wouldn't have been sitting primly

opposite one another in the rugged intimacy of the cabin. She glanced at the narrow bunks, her face suddenly burning with colour as she realised that she was mentally visualising Gray making love on them. But it wasn't Carla's body she visualised entwined with his. It was her own . . .

Where had it come from, this sudden surge of hunger after so many long years of cold uninterest in everything sexual? How had she gained this instinctive knowledge that as a lover Gray would be both demanding and tender? How was it that her very skin seemed to know already what it would be like to experience his touch? It seemed impossible that she, who had known nothing but pain and degradation through the physical side of her marriage, suddenly knew exactly how she could feel in Gray's embrace.

But that knowledge wasn't enough. She wanted the reality of Gray's lovemaking, she wanted . . . She wanted the impossible, she told herself angrily as she cleared up after their alfresco lunch.

Gray was on deck, and she deliberately delayed before going up to join him.

The wind picked up as they headed back, and by mutual consent they concentrated on sailing the sleek yacht.

It was dusk when Gray finally brought her alongside the jetty. The yard was empty, and suddenly, as she unclipped her safety harness, Stephanie realised how utterly exhausted she was.

Perhaps it was that exhaustion that made her clumsy, or perhaps it was another and higher authority that directed her movements.

As she went to follow Gray on to the jetty, a wave

caught the yacht and she lost her balance and fell into the water.

The moment she felt its cold embrace she panicked, forgetting that she could swim, and remembering only that this natural harbour was deep. She heard a splash and then felt an arm tighten round her, and immediately her panic intensified.

She screamed out in fear, gulping in salt water as she fought against that constraining arm. She had to hold on to the boat. She mustn't let go . . . if she did . . . if she did, Paul would let her drown . . .

She screamed again, fighting against the swift, shocking curtain of darkness swooping down on her even as she knew she could not avoid its deathly embrace.

She was lying on the ground. She could feel its hardness underneath her. She was desperately cold and her chest hurt. She shivered and tried to sit up, and was immediately overwhelmed by nausea.

As her stomach rebelled against its intake of salt water she closed her eyes and retched desperately.

Someone was holding her head, speaking to her, but she felt too desperately unwell to respond. As the nausea faded she opened her eyes and saw Gray crouching at her side, watching her.

'All right now . . .' she managed to whisper. 'What happened . . .?'

'You missed the jetty and fell in.'

He was frowning, and soaking wet, she realised, and then memory flooded back, and she remembered for herself what had happened.

'Do you feel well enough to make it to the cottage?'

She nodded her head and struggled to get up, but Gray wouldn't let her, bending to lift her in his arms.

Through the wetness of their clothes she could feel the warmth of his skin, and instinctively she tried to get closer to it. She could feel the hurried thud of his heart as he carried her down the road. Weakly she suppressed a hysterical giggle. If anyone were to see them now . . .

But the road was deserted, and they reached the cottage without incident. Once inside, Gray paused briefly in the hall, without putting her down.

'I'm going to take you upstairs and put you in a hot bath, then I'm going to come down and ring for Doctor Fellows . . .'

Immediately Stephanie felt panic shudder through her. She remembered that Doctor Fellows had seen her after Paul's death. He had prescribed tranquillisers for her, but she had never taken them. She didn't want to see him now.

'No . . . No doctor,' she managed to croak, her throat sore from the salt and sickness. 'I'm all right, Gray. Promise me, no doctor.'

Her panic showed in her eyes and he frowned. She seemed to be all right. It had given him a shock when she slipped and fell overboard, but that had been nothing to the shock he had received when she had fought against him, calling out Paul's name with terror. Had she thought he was Paul come from a watery grave to claim her? She seemed calm and lucid enough now.

'We'll see how you feel after a hot bath,' he temporised, and she was too shaky and exhausted to argue any further.

Too exhausted, in fact, to raise anything more than a token protest when Gray started to fill the bath and then sat down with her on his lap, undressing her as though she was a helpless child.

There was nothing remotely sexual in his touch, and why should there be? she reflected ruefully, catching a momentary glimpse of herself through the steam obliterating the bathroom mirror.

She hardly represented the epitome of female desirability. Her skin was turning blue and covered in goose-bumps. Her hair was hanging in soaking rats' tails, and her dunking in the sea had made her mascara run in dark streaks over her pale face in a way that made her look like an apology for a circus clown. All in all, hardly a tempting sight!

She sat, completely passive, as Gray stripped off her outer clothes, flinching only briefly when his hand accidentally brushed against the side of her breast. She saw his mouth tighten and wondered what he was thinking. Probably that she was a poor apology for a woman ... and nothing like Carla.

He twisted sideways to turn off the taps and test the water, frowning slightly as he asked curtly, 'Can you manage the rest yourself?'

Since all she had on was her briefs and bra, she nodded her head. He was still wearing his own wet clothes, and must be anxious to get under the healing warmth of the shower himself. She scrambled awkwardly off his lap and reached behind her for the catch of her bra, but her arms ached from the unaccustomed exercise, and her fingers were still numb.

After she had fumbled the fastening twice, Gray made an explosive sound of impatience deep in his throat and turned her round, swiftly dispensing with the recalcitrant fastening. Feeling as chastened as an awkward child, Stephanie stepped out of her briefs and turned to get into the bath.

Gray was standing by the door watching her, a tense, unreadable expression on his face.

All at once she was acutely conscious of her deficiencies and limitations.

Tears of exhaustion and unhappiness burned her eyes, and she wondered if she actually had the strength to get into the warm water.

Any other woman worthy of the name could have managed events better than this. Here she was, alone in a potentially provocative situation with the man she loved, and all she could do was to shiver and move clumsily about as though she had suddenly developed two left feet.

Almost as though concurring with her own opinion of herself, Gray moved impatiently towards her, picking her up bodily, his hands on her waist.

'I don't know if it was a good idea letting you persuade me not to call the doctor. I'm going for a shower, and don't you dare to try and get out of that bath until I come back.'

As he lowered her into the water she had an insane urge to cling to him and beg him not to leave her. She had been through too much in too short a time, and now she was paying for it.

The water lapped blissfully at her chilled skin, and she made a small murmur of pleasure, her movements unconsciously sensual as she wriggled under the warmth.

Gray stood watching her for a moment, his mouth grimly compressed, and she wondered again what he was thinking—probably regretting ever asking her to come down to the estuary in the first place. She had been more of a hindrance than a help, she felt sure.

He opened the door and said brusquely, 'Now remember, don't you dare move until I come back.'

The thick, rough quality of his voice made her look curiously at him. His face was slightly flushed, his eyes very dark. He seemed to be unable to tear his attention away from her breasts. Her throat suddenly went dry. Could he ... did he ...? But then abruptly he looked away, and she knew that the intense desire she thought she had read in the tense line of his body had been nothing more than a product of her own fevered imagination.

And then the door opened and he was gone. Voluptuously she gave herself up to the soothing heat of the water as it turned her skin from blue to warm pink. A great wave of tiredness washed over her but she fought it back, reaching for the shampoo, and vigorously soaping her hair.

An impulse she wasn't sure she wanted to investigate made her add scented bath oil to the water when she topped it up, the heat releasing a delicious smell of roses.

She was out of the bath and wrapped in a huge, warm towel when Gray came back.

He frowned when he saw that she had disobeyed his instructions. 'I thought I told you to stay put?'

Stephanie smiled tremulously at him. He was barefoot, wearing a towelling robe that exposed the crisp, damp hair curling on his chest.

'I'm all right now, Gray, I promise you. I'm hungry as well,' she told him, watching the frown disappear and relief take its place.

In actual fact she was feeling exhausted, but the

memory of those moments when she had actually thought she was back with Paul and he was trying to drown her were still too strong and she didn't want to be alone with them.

'All right. You get dressed. I'll go down and light the fire and make us both something to eat.'

She was too exhausted to make much of an effort, simply pulling on clean briefs, and an all-in-one peach jumpsuit with buttons down the front and an elasticated waistband.

Sliding sandals on to her feet, she combed through her wet hair and left it, knowing that it would dry quickly in the heat of the fire.

As she went downstairs she could hear Gray in the kitchen. He had closed the sitting-room curtains, and flames from the burning logs illuminated the attractively furnished room.

Stephanie extinguished the main lights and switched on two lamps. Immediately the room took on an air of intimacy. She heard Gray behind her and swung round, watching his eyebrows draw together as he studied the subdued lighting queryingly.

'My eyes are a bit sore. It must have been the salt water ... the main light's too bright.'

'It's all right, Stephanie. You don't have to make any excuses to me,' he told her roughly, putting the tray down on a small table and cutting right across her stammered explanations. 'After all, we both know you're hardly likely to have set the scene with anything intimate in mind, don't we?'

There was a barbed quality to his words, an acid backlash, almost as though he wanted to hurt her, and he had. Her nerves quivered painfully under his flint-eyed scrutiny and she wanted to cry out in protest that she couldn't help it if she wasn't Carla.

Instead she looked blindly at the supper he had prepared and said huskily, 'Is there anything to drink? Wine? Somehow tonight I don't think I'm going to find it easy to sleep.'

She saw his eyebrows go up, his voice terse as he said curtly, 'I'll go and get a bottle from the kitchen, although if you really think that you should have let me phone the doctor.'

'No, I couldn't take any more tranquillisers, Gray. They remind me too much of . . .'

'Of Paul,' he said, suddenly grabbing hold of her arm in an almost painful grip. 'What happened to you today, Stephanie? Did you think he had come back from the dead to claim you?'

She went white with shock and pain. She couldn't believe this was actually Gray speaking to her like this, with bitterness and contempt.

He released her almost immediately, swearing under his breath, and she watched him blankly as he opened the door.

She was still standing in the same spot when he returned with a bottle of wine and two glasses.

'It's red,' he told her curtly. 'I hope that's all right.'

She shrugged, not really caring, too hurt to make any comment as her mind still grappled with the shock of his verbal attack on her.

He had heated up the chilli left from the previous night and it was deliciously warming, but Stephanie was in no mood to appreciate its spicy taste. She gulped down her wine, and poured herself a second glass. She was thirsty—a legacy from her intake of salt water, no doubt.

The intimacy of the room seemed to have been replaced by a brooding silence. Gray was watching her in a way that unnerved her, although she couldn't have said why.

She saw him frown slightly and make to check her as she drained her second glass of wine. It was smooth, filling her with pleasant heat, driving away the ghosts that haunted her.

'Do you think you ought to have any more?' he asked her drily when she reached for the bottle again.

She never normally drank more than the odd glass, but now she pushed out her bottom lip as rebelliously as any child and said huskily, 'Why not—after all, I'm not going anywhere, am I?'

'You could regret it in the morning,' he warned her, but made no move to stop her from refilling her glass.

In point of fact she was already beginning to feel distinctly hazy, but she welcomed the woolly anaesthetising sensation.

Gray had finished his meal and he watched in silence as she toyed with what was left of her chilli. He had bought in a pot of coffee and he poured them both a cup. She ignored hers, drinking her wine instead.

He waited until she was half-way down it before taking it away from her. 'I think you've had enough of that, don't you?'

She wanted to protest, but the room was swaying disconcertingly around her.

She tried to stand up and sat down again almost immediately, as she felt the floor tilt beneath her feet.

'Why did you think I was Paul, Stephanie?'

Gray's quiet voice seemed to reach her from a long way away. She opened her eyes wide and tried to focus on him.

'Because it was like it was before when he tried to drown me,' she said calmly, proud of the way she managed not to slur her words. She smiled at Gray in her pride, but he wasn't smiling back. In fact, the icy look in his eyes almost dissipated her alcoholic daze.

'Paul tried to *drown* you?'

Didn't he believe her? She frowned in indignation. 'Yes, when we were out sailing. He swung round to quickly and I went overboard. I held on to the side, but he tried to prise my fingers away. I was frightened.' Suddenly her face crumpled and she shivered. 'The coastguards came, and Paul let me get back on board. He wanted to kill me, Gray. He wanted to kill me.'

She repeated the words in a whisper, her brain suddenly clearing of the wine fumes, her expression stark with remembered pain and fear.

'Oh, my God!'

She heard the words and felt their anguish, and then suddenly she was in his arms and he was cradling her trembling body, murmuring soft words of comfort against her ear. She was sobbing out her terror against the warmth of his throat, letting the heat and security of his body engulf her.

'*Why* did you never tell me this before?'

'I couldn't ... I couldn't tell anyone what our marriage was ... I wasn't even sure myself. I used to dream about it after ... after Paul was drowned ... and I sometimes thought I was making excuses for myself ... trying to give myself a reason for not loving him any more.'

'He hated me, Gray. He really hated me towards the end. He wanted to be free. We should never have got married . . .' Her voice died away and she felt a tremendous sense of release sweep through her. She yawned tiredly and stretched in Gray's arms, burrowing into his warmth, suddenly exhausted.

Her eyelashes fluttered down, her eyes closing.

'I think it's time you were in bed.'

She could feel the reverberations of his voice deep in his chest and she snuggled closer to him, giggling deliciously. 'Only if you promise to come with me.'

She felt the tension invade his body, but her own was still too affected by the aftermath of her ordeal and the wine she had drunk to be aware either of what she had said or Gray's reaction to it.

'You're going to regret this in the morning.'

She opened her eyes wide and smiled up at him, seeing her image reflected in the dense blue depths of his, as his eyes darkened and his pupils dilated as though he was held fast in the toils of some intense emotion.

He stood up with her and she curled her arms around his neck, smiling sleepily as he carried her upstairs.

Her room was warm, and when Gray pushed back the bedclothes and sat her down on her bed, she refused to let him go.

'You've got to get undressed,' he reminded her, his eyes narrowing slightly as he added sardonically, 'if you can.'

If she could? What on earth did he mean, of course she could! She'd show him.

Her fingers fumbled over the buttons of her jumpsuit, suddenly seeming ridiculously unable to obey the command of her brain. She heard Gray make a snort of ironic sound beneath his breath as he pushed her fingers away.

'Here, let me. You'll never get out of the thing, the state you're in right now. I should have known better than to let you drink three glasses of that wine. You'll have to manage your own underwear, although I don't suppose it will do you any harm to sleep in . . .' His voice was silenced abruptly as he eased down the top of her jumpsuit, and saw for himself that she was unlikely to face any problems removing her underwear, since all she was wearing was a pair of minute silky briefs.

For a moment he could only stare at the smooth perfection of her body, her skin warm and supple now; her feminine shape reminding him tantalisingly of how long it had been since he had held a woman in his arms.

He was past the age when he could enjoy sex simply for sex's sake. Unable to share his life with the woman he wanted, his conscience hadn't allowed him to give false encouragement to the ones who would have liked to take her place. He could feel the blood beating through his veins, feel the heat building up inside him. He breathed deeply, feeling the pain of his cramped lungs. He wanted her so much, and Paul and her love for him no longer came between them.

With a sudden gesture of revulsion he moved back from the bed. Sensing that he was about to leave her, Stephanie reached out and clutched his arm, her eyes pleading with him not to go.

'Don't leave me, Gray,' she begged huskily. 'Please stay with me, I need you.'

For a moment he let the words fill his senses, drinking them in, absorbing them greedily into his heart, and then reality intruded. She wanted him as a *friend*. She was more than a little tipsy, and hardly knew what she was saying.

'Stephanie, no . . . I . . .' His voice was rough with all that he dared not betray to her, and the harshness of it brought weak tears to her eyes.

Stephanie heard him swear and then say thickly, 'For God's sake, don't cry. You don't know what you're *asking* me, what you're *doing*!'

'I can't bear to be alone tonight.' She was really crying in earnest now and he felt his resolve weakening.

'You lie down. I'll be back in a minute.'

With those few words he had committed himself and he knew he could not go back on that commitment—did not want to go back on it.

Alarm thrilled through Stephanie. He was lying to her, trying to soothe her. He *was* going to leave her and he wouldn't come back. She cried out in protest and clutched desperately at him.

'No . . . no . . . you mustn't go.'

In a voice almost suffocated with anguish Gray said harshly in protest, 'Stephanie, I'm not wearing a damn thing under this robe. I *can't* stay with you like this.'

She was beyond listening to reason, driven almost insane with the fear that still haunted her, and it showed in her face and eyes. She whimpered helplessly and clung to him, pleading with him not to leave her, babbling that she was frightened that if he did Paul would come back.

One part of her brain knew that she was exaggerating and that she really wanted him to stay because she wanted him close to her, because she wanted to have this one night, even if it was all only a pretence; but she refused to heed it, and Gray, with a sudden, savage exclamation of despair, gave in.

'All right, I'll stay,' he told her grimly, reaching out to snap off the lamp and plunge the room into darkness.

He had kept his robe on, Stephanie felt the roughness of the towelling brush her arm as he slid into the bed next to her and pulled up the covers.

She felt him begin to turn away from her and instinctively snuggled closer to him, wrapping herself around him with a determination she could never have shown when she was quite sober.

Part of her registered the shock go through him as Gray felt the warmth of her body against his own, but before he could protest she begged in a tremulous whisper, 'I just want you to hold me, Gray. Please, just hold me.'

He wasn't proof against such a plea. With a groan of submission he turned round and took her in his arms, pillowing her head against his shoulder.

He could smell the clean, fresh shampoo scent of her hair and the faint rose fragrance that still clung to her skin. Beneath his fingertips her body felt like silk. He wanted to touch her so badly . . . to drive out for ever her memories of Paul.

It was bliss, sheer bliss being held in Gray's arms like this, thought Stephanie, even with the thick blanketing fabric of his robe between them, preventing her from enjoying the sensual delight of feeling his flesh against her own.

Stephanie scarcely knew what had happened to her. It was as though another, different Stephanie had suddenly stepped out from behind the old, a Stephanie who knew instinctively all that it meant to be a woman; a Stephanie who ached for the touch of the man she

loved, who felt no fear or inhibitions about expressing
such feelings; the Stephanie she might have been had
she never married Paul.

She felt positively light-headed, delirious almost; and
dangerously free of all past repressions.

The wine still sang dizzily in her veins; she tugged
impatiently at the lapel of Gray's robe and trembled as
her fingertips encountered the male heat of his skin. She
felt the silky texture of the hair on his chest and stroked
her fingertips through it until the tie belt of his robe
prevented her from going any further. Dreamily she
dragged her nails lightly back again, excitement
spiralling through her as she heard Gray's indrawn gasp
of protest, and his hand clamped down over hers,
trapping it against his body.

'*What* the hell do you think you're doing?'

His voice sounded thick and unsteady. Beneath her
hand she could feel the wild pounding of his heart.

Her fingertip touched the hardness of his small, flat
nipple and he groaned out loud, pushing her flat against
the bed and leaning over her, his face contorted in an
expression of savage rage.

Poised above her in the darkness, he reminded her of
a pagan god. She felt small, fragile and unbelievably
feminine, and all her instincts told her that despite his
anger she had aroused him.

She ignored the tiny voice that reminded her that he
loved Carla; she ignored the cautionary voice of
warning telling her not to do anything she would regret.
His fingers still manacled her wrists either side of her
throat where he had pinned her to the bed as he pushed
her away from him. She could see his chest rising and
falling as he breathed raggedly. His body, where it was

exposed by the gap in his robe, gleamed slightly as though it was damp.

'Stephanie, I can't ...' He leaned closer to her, his anger starting to fade, and without even thinking of the consequences she lifted her head and placed her lips delicately against his nipple, enveloping it with their softness and caressing it experimentally with the moist tip of her tongue.

She heard him cry out, a thick, tortured sound that reached her ears, but not her consciousness, which was given over fully to the pleasure of touching him so intimately. When he wrenched away from her, dragging her into a sitting position and holding her at arm's length from him, she felt so acutely deprived that her body ached and trembled.

'Do you *know* what you're doing?'

As though it was someone else who said the words she heard herself replying calmly, 'Yes, I'm touching you the way I want you to touch me. Make love to me, Gray. Make love to me tonight. Let me believe tonight that I'm a desirable woman, that I'm not what Paul said.'

He should stop her. He knew that. She didn't know what she was saying ... what she was asking. She was still in shock, still traumatised by what had happened. He tried to resist the lure of her words, to deny the surge of feeling that poured through him. He had wanted her, loved her, for ten years. But for her sake ... She didn't want him really. She just wanted to exorcise Paul's ghost, to prove to herself that she was finally free. He closed his eyes and remembered the feel of her soft mouth against his body. A hot tide of need convulsed him.

'Gray, I know I'm not Carla . . . but don't reject me, please . . .'

Stephanie heard him groan, a low, tortured sound that tore at her own nerves and she tensed, waiting for the words that would end her secret fantasy of being with this man, being the woman she had never allowed herself to be.

Gray moved, shifting his weight so that he could take her fully in his arms. She shivered in a mixture of shock and delight as she felt his mouth moving against her skin—her forehead, her eyes, her cheek and down her jaw. She tilted her throat eagerly, quivering beneath the hungry ferocity of his kisses as his lips caressed the taut, smooth vulnerability of her skin.

Her head fell back against his arm, her body trembling with frantic pleasure as his mouth closed over the pulse thudding erratically at the base of her throat.

It was beyond her wildest dreams; as though he was as desperately hungry for her as she was for him.

Her fingers scrabbled for purchase against the thickness of the terry robe, and with a thick sound of impatience Gray shrugged his upper torso free of it.

His skin was hot, smooth like satin or velvet, she thought hectically, almost kneading it in her pleasure, tiny muted sounds of delight emerging from her throat.

Gray tilted her head, his mouth moving from her throat to her lips, biting gently and then not so gently at their softness, inflaming her until she wrapped her arms impatiently round him, dragging his head down so that he couldn't pull away.

The sensation of his mouth on hers, his tongue tasting, exploring, and finally thrusting passionately within the softness of hers, was a delight beyond anything she had

known or dreamed of knowing. She clung to him,
offering herself to him with reckless abandon.

His mouth released hers, his thumb rubbing softly
over its swollen contours. His breath filled her ear,
making her squirm in renewed pleasure.

'I want you to touch me the way you were doing
before. I want to feel your mouth against me here,' he
murmured huskily.

She quivered with joy that she could make him want
her touch, scattering eager kisses against his skin until
he moaned and dragged her head down against his
chest, his whole body shuddering as she repeated the
provocative caress she had given him earlier.

The tiny nub of flesh seemed to swell and harden, and
as he cried out her name in a voice rough with need, she
felt her own body swell and tighten almost shockingly.

'See how you make me feel when you touch me like
that? And I'm going to make you feel the same way.'

His voice was thick and unfamiliar, and she shivered
under the sensual rasp of it.

Paul had never particularly enjoyed touching her
breasts. He had been too young and impatient to
indulge in caresses, she recognised now, and then her
whole mind went numb and her body arched in ecstatic
pleasure as she felt Gray's lips against her breast and
then her nipple as it swelled eagerly to meet the raw
heat of his mouth.

The slight drag of his teeth, instead of bringing pain,
brought only a fresh upsurge of pleasure. Her soft
moans were almost lost beneath the harsh staccato of his
breathing as he gave in to the need that had burned in
him for too long, cupping both her breasts in hands that
trembled slightly, pampering their swollen crests with

the erotic lash of his tongue until they were so sensitised that merely to feel the warmth of his breath against her skin was enough to convulse her with the aching need to have his mouth against her body.

The euphoria created by the wine had faded, leaving her completely sober, but it was too late to go back now, Stephanie thought recklessly. At this moment in time she no longer cared that he loved Carla. He was here with her . . . and in her arms, he was hers; he wanted her.

She cried out as his mouth tugged at her breast and she felt the sharp edge of his teeth.

Instantly he released her. 'I'm sorry, I didn't mean to hurt or frighten you . . . I was forgetting . . .'

'Paul never . . .' She swallowed hard, missing the moist contact of his mouth against her skin. 'Paul never wanted to . . . to make love to me like this.'

She heard Gray say something under his breath and then he said, 'I shouldn't be doing this . . .'

'I want you to.' How easy it was to say. 'Neither of us is hurting anyone else by making love, Gray. I need you to make love to me to . . .'

'To what? Free you from the past? Show you that you really are a desirable woman?'

'Both those.' And much much more than he would never know, she tagged on silently. 'I need the memories tonight will give me, I need something to hold on to in the dark days ahead.'

He had turned slightly away from her and she sensed that he was having second thoughts. She shivered and instantly he reached out and touched her comfortingly.

'I . . . I can't promise that I won't hurt you.' His voice sounded oddly strained. 'I'll try not to . . . but it's been a long time for me, too. Do you understand what I'm trying to say?'

She did, and it shocked her. What did he mean by a 'long time'? Surely he and Carla had been lovers at some point; but now was hardly the time to remind him that he loved another woman, nor to dwell on it herself.

'Paul hurt me because he liked hurting me. I was frightened of him, which made me . . .' She felt herself flush as she tried to put into words what she felt. 'I'm not frightened of *you*, Gray. You won't hurt me.'

He made a thick, choking sound in his throat and suddenly she was back in his arms, his hands shaping and moulding her, pulling her hard against him so that she could feel his arousal through the thick folds of his robe.

She moved impatiently against him and felt his chest rise and fall at his quick, indrawn breath. Her fingers encountered the knot fastening his robe and she tugged on it.

'Stephanie, no.' His voice was thick and slurred. 'No . . . not yet. I want to give you all the pleasure you never had with Paul before. I . . .'

His words made her skin prickle with sensual heat, but she still cried out protestingly, 'Gray, I want to feel *all* of you against me. *All* of you.'

She felt him shudder just before he buried his mouth against her skin, tasting the smooth tenderness of her shoulder where it joined her neck. His hand stroked her body, cupping her breasts, spanning her waist and then caressing the feminine curve of her hip before moving to cover the soft swell of her stomach and stroke tantalisingly along the edge of her briefs.

She was torn between wanting to touch him with the

freedom with which he was caressing her, and giving herself up to the pleasure he was inciting. She ached for them both to be completely free of their clothes. The only covering she wanted was the heat of his body.

His hand covered her over the silky fineness of her briefs and she moved protestingly against him, lifting her hips and nipping frantically at the smooth flesh of his shoulder. His hands lifted her, moulded her, pulling her tightly against the hardness of his body, and she sobbed out loud as she twisted against him.

This time her anxious fingers managed to untie the towelling knot and she made a soft, feminine sound of triumph deep in her throat, a feline purring noise that accurately mirrored her feelings as she pushed the robe away and yielded to her need to feel all of him against her.

Only she had forgotten she was still wearing her own briefs. But as she made to remove them with a muted sound of self-disgust, Gray stopped her. 'No . . . let me.'

She quivered expectantly, eager to be held against him, knowing from the arousal of his body that he wanted her as much as she wanted him, but instead, Gray pushed her flat against the bed and arched over her as he eased the silky barrier away.

Impatiently she waited for him to join her, dreading reading in his hesitation that he had changed his mind; that he had remembered that she wasn't Carla.

Dreading feeling him move away from her, she cried out huskily, 'Gray, please I . . .'

'Paul starved you,' he said softly, as though he hadn't heard her. 'He deprived you of love and pleasure. I can't make that up to you, but tonight I want to give you a banquet, the memory of which will stay with you for ever.'

He cupped her heel in the warmth of his palm as he spoke, rubbing it caressingly. Her skin started to tingle as his fingers stroked up her calf and his mouth explored the sensitive hollow behind her knee. His teeth nibbled gently at her inner thigh and she quivered dizzily, her finger-nails digging protestingly into his arm.

'No . . . no, you mustn't,' she cried out weakly, but he ignored her, stroking fingers that were supposed to soothe, but in reality only inflamed, over the taut swell of her stomach.

His hand cupped her and his mouth closed over the swollen areola of her breast, sucking erotically. Her body arched beneath the darts of fire engulfing her, her skin damp with a soft dew of sweat. His fingers stroked and aroused, and she felt herself moving helplessly against them, pierced with such a sweet pleasure that she couldn't help crying out against him.

She could hear Gray breathing, a harsh, laboured sound that betrayed his own arousal. His mouth left her breast and moved hotly over her skin, caressing her stomach, leaving it quivering with nerves, then moving on to her inner thigh.

His hands held her prisoner, as helpless in their grip as she was in the grip of the need aching inside her. She felt his mouth on her body, caressing it with deliberate intimacy and, although she cried out in shock, she couldn't stop herself from responding to its insistent demand.

Ripples of sensation gathered and bunched tightly inside her. Her throat was rigid with tension, her body bathed in moist heat. She had never, ever experienced anything like this with Paul.

As her body began to explode in tiny shock waves of passion she felt Gray move and then lift her, fitting her to the taut hardness of his own.

She absorbed the shock of his first controlled thrust with a sense of awed disbelief, feeling her body soften and expand to welcome the powerful strength of him.

The pain she had known with Paul might never have existed. With each thrust of his body Gray was bringing her to fresh heights of pleasure; fresh knowledge about herself.

She arched eagerly against him, wrapping her arms and legs round him, crying out in spontaneous delight until he took the sound into his mouth, kissing her with an almost feverish intensity that was rapidly mirrored by the uncontrollable surge and demand of his body.

She felt as she had never felt in her life before—powerful, almost mysterious, and yet humble at the same time in the knowledge that she was the one who had aroused him to this pitch; that hers was the body in which he sought release. And then, as the circles of pleasure started to tighten again, she stopped thinking and gave herself over entirely to feeling.

She cried out his name as the world exploded around her, almost delirious with pleasure as she felt his body achieve fulfilment within her own.

It took her a long time to float back down to reality and when she eventually did, she discovered that Gray was fast asleep. She laughed weakly, tears of joy running out of her eyes. Paul had been wrong. She hadn't been frigid. Her heart overflowed with gratitude and love towards the man who had shown her the truth. She wanted to tell him how she felt, but she hesitated to disturb his sleep.

Besides, she was tired herself. She closed her eyes and let her tired body relax. They could talk in the morning.

CHAPTER EIGHT

ONLY in the morning, when Stephanie woke up Gray had gone, and to judge from the coldness on his side of the bed he had been up for quite some time.

And in the cold light of day things seemed rather different. Stephanie's skin burned hotly as she remembered her abandoned response to him. Her response to *him*? She groaned out loud as she remembered begging him to make love to her.

How could she face him? What on earth could she *say*? *How* could she have risked prejudicing their friendship?

She dressed reluctantly and went downstairs.

The scent of freshly brewed coffee led her to the kitchen. Gray was sitting down at the table reading his paper. He looked up as she walked in, his expression cloaked and distant.

Stephanie bit her lip, gnawing at it. There was no easy or polite way round this.

'Do you still want me to stay after . . . after last night?' she asked baldly.

For a moment she thought he wasn't going to reply and then, without looking at her, he said coolly, 'Why not? We both know it wasn't me you were making love with. We both know *why* you felt the need to physically exorcise Paul's ghost. It happened, and if anything, I'm the one to blame. You had been drinking—a notorious relaxer of inhibitions as any number of unfortunate young women will testify. I suggest we both put the entire incident behind us.'

To say that she was shocked was putting it mildly. Whatever she had expected, it certainly hadn't been Gray's cool dismissal of the entire incident as though it was so unimportant as to be barely worthy of comment.

Was this the same man who last night had whispered so passionately to her that he wanted to give her a banquet of passion? Was this the same man who had kissed and stroked every inch of her body, who had . . . Her skin burned, and she shuddered tensely. Gray was right. If they were to continue as friends, she would have to pretend that nothing untoward had ever happened. That was, of course, if she *could*.

'Carla's been on the phone,' Gray continued casually. 'She wanted to remind us that we're expected there for dinner tonight.'

Stephanie went icy cold. So that was why he was trying to pretend nothing had happened between them! He had spoken to Carla, and hearing her voice had no doubt reminded him that *she* was the one he loved.

'Coffee's freshly made if you want some. I'm taking the yacht out again today.' He glanced at his watch. 'In fact I'll have to be on my way in a few minutes.'

'I . . . I'll follow you down to the yard later,' Stephanie told him, fighting hard not to let her voice tremble. This was dreadful, awful . . . impossible. But she mustn't *let* it be impossible, an inner voice warned her. She must somehow find the strength to follow Gray's lead, otherwise she would end up embarrassing them both.

Without looking at him, she went to pour herself a

cup of coffee. As he watched the downbent vulnerability of her exposed neck, Gray slowly unclenched his
tightly closed fist. Last night she had given herself to
him so freely . . . so innocently . . . he dared not scare her
away by telling her just how much it had meant to him.
He had woken up this morning and ached to make love
to her again, but he had let her sleep on. When she
remembered what had happened between them, would
she blame him? She had been suffering from both shock
and too much wine on an empty stomach. After the way
Paul had treated her it was not surprising that she would
want to prove her own sexuality. He didn't deceive
himself that she felt any particular attraction for him.
She trusted him. She looked on him as a friend, or at
least she had done until last night. Maybe in time she
might come to feel something more. He mustn't rush
her, and yet when he remembered how she had felt in
his arms, he ached to pick her up and take her back to
bed, and keep her there until she moaned against his
skin in the way she had done last night; frantic,
passionate little moans of need.

Stephanie tensed as she heard Gray's chair scrape
back. He didn't even look at her as he walked to the
kitchen door. She ached to go after him, to . . .

To what? she asked herself derisively. To tell him
that I love him? Hadn't she already laid enough
burdens on him?

The day dragged, and it didn't help that she was both
physically and emotionally exhausted. The very last
thing she wanted was to have to share Gray with anyone
at all this evening, least of all with the woman he loved.

She couldn't even frame the words within her mind without them hurting her, but she made herself do it. There was no point in hiding from the truth. Gray loved Carla. Oh, he loved her, too . . . as a friend.

At four o'clock there was a sudden flurry of telephone calls and enquiries, and it was almost six before she was free to leave the yard.

The yacht was already tied up at the jetty, signalling that Gray was back. He must have returned while she was busy in the back office, and it hurt that he had gone straight back to the cottage without stopping off to see her.

He was on the telephone when she walked into the cottage, and he replaced the receiver as she came in. With a twist of pain in her heart Stephanie recognised the constraint between them. She wondered if he had been talking to Carla; if he felt guilty about last night because he felt he had betrayed the woman he loved.

As she was beginning to discover, no one act or incident could be taken in isolation; everything in life interlocked or reflected on everything else. She had wanted to keep her memories of last night shining and untarnished, but already she was recognising that to do so would be next to impossible.

'You look pale, are you feeling all right?' Gray frowned as he looked at her. 'You know you don't have to come tonight, if you'd rather not . . .'

She read in his eyes the message that he would rather she did not come, and instantly she was on fire with jealousy.

Her voice burned with acid as she responded angrily, 'Surely that would defeat the whole purpose of either of us going? Unless, of course, Carla has had a change of heart and is now prepared to leave Alex for you?'

'No, she won't leave him.'

Shrugging, Stephanie countered curtly, 'Then it would be better if I were there, wouldn't it? You don't want Alex getting suspicious at this stage, with the Fastnet so close.'

She thought she saw a flicker of shame darken Gray's eyes, and for a moment she longed to reach out and comfort him, but her hand fell away even as she raised it, her pale face flushing as she realised how open to misinterpretation any gesture of affection on her part might be now.

'We're due there at seven,' she said instead. 'I'd better go up and change. How formal an occasion will it be?'

'As formal as any dinner party you might attend in London,' Gray advised her coolly, almost as though they were enemies and not friends.

The dress she chose was black, underlining her mood as well as the pallor of her skin. It made a striking contrast to her rich chestnut hair, and with it she wore silk stockings and high-heeled shoes. The dress was a Jean Muir in heavy silk jersey, cut to mould and flatter her shape. She was too tired and depressed to do anything with her hair other than catch it back with tortoiseshell combs. Large, pearl costume-jewellery earrings edged with *diamanté* added a subtle touch of glitter. Blusher, eyeshadow and lip gloss warmed the too-pale translucence of her skin, and then she was ready.

Her dress had long sleeves and the evening was warm enough for her not to need a jacket.

Gray was waiting for her downstairs and her heart lurched as she studied him surreptitiously. He looked as much at ease in his dinner suit as he did in his jeans. He glanced at his watch and she caught the discreet flash of gold cuff-links at his wrists. He looked up and saw her, and his eyes seemed to darken and burn. She ached to fling herself into his arms and be held close against his body, but she forced herself to smile carelessly and take her time about joining him.

They drove to the Farlows' house in silence. For the first time that she could remember she had to suppress the nervous inclination to make small talk to cover the silence between them.

The Farlows lived in an attractive Georgian house several miles outside the village. It had its own drive, illuminated with traditionally styled lights that revealed the beginnings of a smooth sweep of immaculate lawn. Ivy covered the end wall of the house, giving it a settled, comfortable air.

Before Gray stopped the car she caught a glimpse of an attractive conservatory and was momentarily pierced with envy for Carla. She already had so much, and now Gray's love as well. She told herself she was being bitchy for guessing that Carla would be reluctant to give up such a beautiful home, but when Carla opened the door to them and welcomed them both with equal warmth and enthusiasm, Stephanie told herself that her bitchiness was well justified.

A woman who could greet her lover in the presence of her husband, so free of guilt and self-consciousness, had to have a core of heartlessness. But as she led them into their comfortable drawing-room and Alex served them with drinks, Carla was so pleasant and natural with them both that Stephanie found it impossible not to warm to her. She dared not look at Gray when Carla voluntarily produced studio portraits of their two children.

'I miss them dreadfully,' she confided to Stephanie, 'but we haven't lived here very long, and I agree with Alex that it would have been wrong to disrupt their schooling. Hopefully, now that we're settled here, next year I'll be able to find them both good day schools locally.'

The two men had drawn away and from the snatches of conversation Stephanie caught were deep in a discussion about the boat.

Something of her feelings must have shown in her expression because Carla touched her arm lightly, and said quietly, 'I know how you must feel, but try not to worry. Gray isn't the sort of man to take unnecessary risks.'

For a moment Stephanie bristled; longing to tell Carla that there was nothing she could tell her about Gray, and then the ambiguity of the other woman's statement struck her and she longed to demand to know how a man who did not take unnecessary risks had managed to fall in love with his partner's wife.

She still believed quite passionately that Gray would never have fallen in love with Carla without encouragement, and then a traitorous little voice whispered tormentingly to her, 'Why not? You did ... with him ...'

'The Fastnet is one of the most dangerous sea races there is,' she retorted to cover her own inner turmoil.

'Not so very long ago many lives were lost, and boats abandoned.'

'Yes, I know.' Carla looked at her and said quietly, 'Alex's brother was one of them. That's why Alex is so determined that this boat will be both successful and safe. Alex and David, his brother, designed and built the boat that was lost. Alex should have sailed in it, but almost at the last minute he broke his leg and couldn't go.' Her face clouded as though she was remembering great unhappiness, and against her will Stephanie felt a confused sort of compassion for her.

'I'll never forget his face when we got the news that David was lost. I promise you, Stephanie, that Gray will be safe.'

'Hey, what are you two girls talking about so seriously?' Alex interrupted them, adding with a teasing grin at Carla, 'I don't know about everyone else, but I'm starving.'

Altogether it was a very confusing evening, Stephanie decided. If she had met them without knowing of Carla's relationship with Gray, if she hadn't been aware that Carla couldn't possibly genuinely love her husband, she would have thought them an exceedingly happy couple and she would have thoroughly enjoyed their company. Both of them had a lively interest in the arts, and far from centring exclusively on sailing and the Fastnet the conversation covered a wide range of diverse subjects. Of all of them she seemed to be the only one who was ill at ease.

It was while they were drinking their coffee that Alex unknowingly dropped his bombshell.

'I've chartered the *Nemesis* again this summer, since

you enjoyed it so much last year, Carla.'

'The *Nemesis* is a ten-berth schooner moored in St Lucia that we chartered last year,' he explained to Stephanie. 'All four of us went and we fully enjoyed the experience. There's plenty of space and we'd love you both to join us this time.'

Stephanie felt her face go stiff with shock and suspicion. Was Carla behind this? Was this her way of ensuring that she had the company of both her lover and her husband?

One look at Gray's face assured Stephanie that he was as surprised by Alex's announcement as she had been herself but, to her shock, instead of instantly rejecting the offer he said quietly, 'That's very generous of you, Alex. I'd love to join you, but of course it's up to Steph.'

With all three of them focusing on her, Stephanie had little option but to swallow her ire and say huskily, 'Yes, it is generous of you. I'm sure I'll love it.'

How could Gray have acceded so easily to Alex's suggestion? she wondered miserably. He must *know* the temptation he would be facing in the close confines of the schooner. How on earth would he be able to endure being so close to Carla, knowing she was with Alex?

In his shoes . . . in his shoes, she couldn't have endured to watch him with another woman. It was tearing her apart being here tonight. Every time he looked at Carla, every time he spoke to her, she was consumed with jealousy.

Irrationally, as she listened to the three of them making plans for the projected holiday, she was filled with resentment. How on earth could either Carla or Alex believe that she and Gray were lovers, when he was practically ignoring her?

'You're very quiet.' Carla smiled at her, and once again Stephanie was struck by the friendly naturalness of the other woman's smile. Had she not seen for herself the faint hauteur and coldness in Carla's attitude towards her the first time they met, had she not known the truth about her relationship with Gray, she might almost have found herself liking the other woman, and that confused and distressed her.

'I'm afraid I'm rather tired,' she responded unevenly. 'Gray took me sailing yesterday, and I'm still suffering the after-effects of all that fresh air.'

Instantly she was aware of the covert look that Gray and Carla exchanged, and again she was filled with jealousy.

How *could* Alex not notice the intimacy of that shared glance?

'I'm afraid Stephanie isn't the only one who's tired,' Gray commented. 'Would you think us very provincial if we make an early night of it?'

Carla and Alex accompanied them to the front door and watched until they were both installed in the car.

Stephanie sat rigidly in her seat, aching with jealousy and tension. Last night Gray had made love to her, but tonight that intimacy might never have been.

She sat in stiff silence as he drove them back to the cottage, getting out of the Range Rover the moment it stopped.

She had intended to be upstairs and in her own room before Gray came in, too angry at what she saw as his weakness over Carla to want to talk to him, but her throat was dry, and she stopped for a glass of water.

He came in while she was still drinking it, and waited until she had put the glass down before taking both her hands in his and holding them gently.

'Stephanie, what is it? You've been tense and on edge all evening. If it's because of last night . . .'

Instantly she was furious both with him and with herself. 'No, it's not because of last night,' she told him tight-lipped. 'It's because of tonight. Because of the way you weakly fell in with Alex's plans. You told me that you wanted to break away from Carla, that you *knew* that you had no future with her. And yet tonight you couldn't wait to accept their invitation to join them in the Caribbean.'

She watched as his forehead furrowed.

'No . . . no, Stephanie, you've got it all wrong. Let me explain.'

'I don't *need* any explanations, or any lies, Gray. I can see for myself what's going on,' she told him bitterly. 'I offered to help you by pretending that you and I . . . that we were lovers because I thought you genuinely meant it when you said it was all over between you and Carla. I won't be used as a convenient screen behind which you can carry on your adulterous relationship.' Her voice was thick with biting scorn, but to her surprise Gray looked more angry than contrite.

'I am *not* having an affair with Carla,' he ground out furiously. 'Surely last night showed you that much?'

She felt as though her whole body was on fire. How *could* he refer to what they had shared last night in the same sentence as his affair with a married woman? Only to him, Carla wasn't a married woman; she was the woman he loved, she acknowledged miserably.

'I don't want to talk about last night,' she told him, childishly snatching her hands away and heading for the door. 'I'd like to forget that it ever happened.'

She was lying of course, but even so her voice rang with intensity and conviction. Gray couldn't see her face, or the tears filling her eyes. He had hurt her tonight and badly, and she wanted to hurt him in turn, she acknowledged unhappily as she headed for her room. Although how any comment of hers could hurt him, when he was so obviously concerned only with Carla, she really did not know.

CHAPTER NINE

FOR a week they shared the cottage together in an atmosphere of subdued hostility. Too proud and too hurt to back down from the stance she had adopted, Stephanie continued to treat Gray with coldness although inwardly she ached to go back to the days when they had been close.

Even his friendship seemed to be lost to her now, and several times she thought of suggesting she should leave, but she was frightened to do so, dreading hearing him agree.

It was hell living with him like this, but it would be even greater hell to be sent away.

The week stretched to ten days, time running out swifter than a rip tide as the date of the Fastnet approached.

Gray was gone most days now, testing and re-testing the boat. Hostility gave way to a cool state of armed neutrality. When he came home in the evening she asked him about the yacht's progress, but the old spontaneity of their relationship was gone. She knew that she was losing weight, growing increasingly tense.

As far as she knew Gray hadn't seen Carla since the evening of the dinner party, and part of her urged her to apologise and take back her hasty words, but she was still too hurt and jealous.

Added to that was her ever-increasing anxiety as the

days dribbled away and the race loomed ominously close at hand.

Several times she sensed Gray's frustration with the cool barrier she had put up against him, but every time he tried to recapture their earlier closeness she froze him off, panicked by the fear that if she let him get emotionally close to her again she would break down completely and reveal to him how she felt.

Once she would have said, if asked, that there was nothing she could not tell Gray, but now that had changed.

The weekend before the commencement of the Fastnet they were invited to an official pre-start party at a prestigious local yacht club, along with other entrants in the race.

Carla and Alex were also going, and on a reckless impulse Stephanie went into Southampton and spent far more than she had intended on a peach satin ballgown that did amazing things for her hair and skin.

On the suggestion of the sales assistant she also made an appointment to have her hair done in a profusion of vaguely eighteenth-century curls to compliment the formality of her gown.

Her impulsive decision to buy a new dress and have her hair done meant that she didn't arrive back at the cottage until later than she had planned.

Gray was already upstairs getting ready and she hurried into her own bedroom and quickly started getting changed.

To compliment the narrow, stiffened bodice of her dress, the saleswoman had recommended that she wear a lacy, boned basque underneath to ensure a smooth fit, and she had just finished struggling into this instrument of torture and securing fine white stockings to the attached suspenders when Gray knocked briefly on the door.

Conscious that time was running out, and her mind on the stamina of those women of long ago who submitted to being pushed and squeezed into real corsets, she forgot to respond.

When her bedroom door suddenly opened and Gray strode in, she didn't know which one of them was the more shocked.

Gray took one look at her supple, white, lace-clad body and immediately went completely still, while all she could think of was how ridiculously and deliberately provocative she must look clad in nothing but high-heeled sandals, stockings, briefs and an article of underwear that seemed to make her waist look far smaller than it had ever appeared before, and contra-dictorarily her breasts surely far fuller.

'I . . . I wasn't sure if you were back,' Gray said at last, averting his eyes from her.

'I'm sorry I'm so late.' Her fingers touched the tumbled mass of dark red curls that had been the cause of the delay. 'I bought a new dress for tonight, and then I had to have my hair done . . .'

She was babbling and she knew it, but she felt so ridiculously self-conscious. Gray was already dressed. The party was a formal one, with white tie specified.

'I've only got to do my face and put on my dress. I'm leaving it until last because the skirts are so full. I . . .' She was babbling again, she realised, and she checked herself, a sudden surge of warmth invading her body as she saw Gray look at her.

'With skin like yours you don't need make-up,' he told

her abruptly and she was conscious of a fresh surge of heat. It was almost as though he was actually touching her, smoothing and savouring the softness of her flesh as he had done the night they had made love.

'What time did you order the taxi for?' Somehow she had to break the heavy silence hanging over them.

'You've got just under half an hour.' He paused and looked at her again slowly before retreating and closing the door. After he had gone, Stephanie put her hands against her flushed face, her colour deepening even further as she saw her own reflection in the mirror.

Against the soft white of her basque and stockings, her skin glowed creamy warm. Her eyes seemed to have gone darker, almost slumbrous, and the way the stylist had done her hair gave her, even to her own eyes, an unexpected air of sensuality. Was *that* how Gray had seen her? Or when he had looked at her had he only seen Carla?

Impatient and angry with herself she quickly put on her make-up, applying it only slightly less dextrously than usual. Her dress came last and she stepped into it, grimacing as she battled with the mass of net underskirts. The three-quarter sleeves could be worn on or off the shoulders, and she left them down as she reached behind herself to slide up the zip, only when it got to her waist it wouldn't go any further, no matter how much she struggled.

In the shop she had commented on how close-fitting it was, but the assistant had assured her that a close fit on such a gown was essential. She, Stephanie remembered now, had had both hands free to close the fastener. Frightened of breaking it completely in her impatience, she stuffed her evening bag with what she would need for the evening and opened the door.

Hurrying downstairs was impossible with such wide, heavy skirts, but finally she made it. She found Gray in the sitting-room.

'I can't get the zip up properly,' she told him without preamble. 'It needs two hands. Can you do it for me?'

She turned her back to him as she spoke, breathing in sharply as she felt his hands on her back.

After all her struggles it seemed unfair that the zip should slide home easily and immediately under Gray's calm hands, and she let out her breath in a jerky sigh as he closed the small top fastener for her.

The dress was quite low at the back, and cut in such a way at the front that it exposed the soft upper curves of her breasts. Conscious that Gray was looking at her as she turned round, she asked huskily, 'Well, what do you think?'

'I can't decide whether you look more beautiful with it on or off,' he said slowly at last, 'but at least now I know the reason for that amazingly sexy piece of underwear you're wearing.'

He was actually teasing her, Stephanie realised, her spirits lightening as she responded lightly, 'Ah, but you weren't supposed to see that.'

'No, I don't think I should have done,' Gray agreed huskily. 'The memory of seeing you in it is likely to cause me to keep awake at nights, Stephanie.'

He looked at her broodingly, and she held her breath, wondering what he intended to say. The sharp ring of the doorbell shattered the silence and Gray frowned.

'Damn, that will be the taxi.'

The party would have been one of the most enjoyable she had ever attended had it not been for her continuing anxiety over the Fastnet race and the misery of her own incredibly foolish love for Gray.

He danced with her most of the evening, holding her as close as the full skirts of her gown would allow, and at midnight, when balloons were released from the ceiling and everyone toasted the success of the Race he swung her into his arms and kissed her with passion and something almost approaching violence, holding her against his body long after most of the other revellers had drifted apart.

The fierce passion of that kiss stayed with her on the drive home. Was it the frustration, or his need for Carla that had driven him into her arms? She would not be used as a substitute for the other woman, no matter how much she loved him, but even as she made that determined vow, she knew that if he touched her, if he kissed her, she might not be able to resist him.

Nervous tension kept her wide awake and restless on the ride home. Once inside the cottage, habit made her ask Gray if he would like a nightcap.

'Not for me,' he told her abruptly. 'I think I'll go up.'

His retreat from her, after she had half expected him to at least attempt to make love to her, brought her down to earth with shattering speed. It was no use telling herself that Gray was acting honourably in removing temptation from them both; it was no use telling herself that she would not have wanted him to make love to her while craving another woman.

As she prepared for bed, all she could think of was how he had looked at her earlier in the evening; how he had held and kissed her, and how much she ached to have him with her now.

* * *

The morning of the Fastnet dawned bright and clear. Stephanie went with Carla and Alex to see Gray off. She was a mass of nerves, so tense that even her bones seemed to ache with it.

Gray kissed her briefly before going on board, a hard, all-too-short embrace that left her aching and alone.

'Don't worry about him. He'll be fine,' Alex reassured her as they waited for the starting signal. 'You wait and see.'

They watched until Gray's boat was just a distant speck before joining the other onlookers drifting away.

Carla and Alex invited her to go back with them, but she shook her head. There was work to do at the yard; work which would keep her occupied physically if not mentally. As always when she saw Carla, she was confused by her own ambivalent feelings towards the other woman, unable to escape from the knowledge that in other circumstances she would have liked her.

It was all so easy to understand why Gray loved her, and it was equally hard to equate the Carla who appeared to be a devoted and loving wife with the Carla she knew to have cheated on her husband.

All day she barely moved out of range of the radio, like everyone else working in the yard.

So far the weather was ideal, but Stephanie was haunted by memories of the tragic outcome of the Fastnet race only years before.

The news bulletin on television that evening showed that Gray was well to the forefront of the race. He had been interviewed by local television the week before and this interview was now re-run.

Stephanie felt her stomach muscles clench as she fought against a wave of longing to be with him as she looked at his familiar and beloved face.

Time dragged, losing all real meaning. She couldn't sleep, waking almost hourly to check on the radio bulletins.

All day she was lethargic and tense. Luckily, the yard was not too busy, apart from callers coming to enquire about Gray and his boat following the item on TV.

Gray had been right, Stephanie decided as she left the yard that evening; his entry in the race *had* indeed caused an upsurge of interest in the yard.

The week dragged on, her sleepless nights beginning to take their toll.

Carla rang her almost every day, solicitous and concerned for her; more like a good and close friend than the woman who was her rival. She was invited to their house several times, but she refused, knowing that she was hardly likely to be a social asset in her present anxious mood.

Gray was still among the lead yachts, and they were now in the dangerous seas round Ireland.

At last her sleepless nights took their toll, and she woke one morning having slept heavily and dreamlessly to the news that one of the lead yachts in the race had capsized, with the loss of at least one member of the crew.

Gray's yacht was one of the smallest ones in the race—he was its sole crew—and she expelled a taut sigh of relief as she realised the damaged boat could not be his.

Even so, the accident increased her anxiety. The weather was changing, growing more dangerous, and there were reports of heavy seas and other yachts in trouble.

On the last day of the race, Gray and three other yachts were in the lead, but they were encountering heavy seas, and the helicopter carrying the TV crew following the race had reported that conditions were fast becoming dangerous.

Just before lunchtime a bulletin on the radio announced that another boat had capsized, with no sign of any life on board. The announcement was followed by the information that the Air Sea Rescue were searching for the one-man crew of the yacht *Good Hope*, sailed by Gray ...

Stephanie went cold and clung desperately to her desk as she listened with disbelieving ears to what she had dreaded hearing all along.

Gray's boat had overturned and Gray was lost at sea. She knew all too well what that meant, and if the Air Sea Rescue team had not found him already, then there was scant hope for his survival, unless he had been picked up by another contestant.

Almost immediately the phone rang, and although she knew it would probably be Carla she didn't answer it. The pain of what she was feeling was unendurable, intolerable, almost unbelievable, as though somehow it wasn't quite real and that soon she would be able to open her eyes and discover that it was all part of some dreadful nightmare.

There was no one in the yard as she walked through it like someone in a trance, heading almost automatically for the narrow path that followed the coast.

It had started to rain, and the wind was cold, gathering in force as it swept in from the sea, but Stephanie ignored it. She could barely feel the icy sting of rain on her skin for the greater pain in her heart.

Gray was gone . . . lost . . . drowned as Paul had been; and in her overwrought state she felt as though *she* had been the one to cause his death; as though she had brought him bad luck by loving him. She was crying without realising it, hot tears pouring down her cold cheeks, her body shivering convulsively, locked in the grip of intense pain.

How long she walked she didn't know. It began to grow dark, and her body hurt. She had walked almost in a complete circle, along the estuary, over the mouth of the river, then down the other side, and now she was almost back in the village. The walk had exhausted her physically, but mentally . . . Walking had done nothing to ease her inner pain.

As she approached the cottage she saw that the lights were on, and she shuddered, anticipating the ordeal that lay ahead.

When Paul had drowned, Gray had shielded her from all the formalities, protecting and cosseting her from the reality of what had happened, but there was no one to protect her now.

They would all be there, the police, other authorities . . . the Press, somehow they must have found a way into the house. The police, she supposed tiredly, reluctantly approaching the back door and pushing it open.

The kitchen was empty. They would all be in the sitting-room, she thought, numbly crossing the hall.

As she reached for the sitting-room door-handle it turned from the other side. She stepped back, waiting. The door opened and Gray emerged, his black hair tousled, his face drawn in lines of exhaustion.

For a moment she stood rooted to the spot, unable to move, unable to believe the evidence of her own eyes, and then with a sob of relief she flung herself into his arms and felt them close round her.

'Gray . . . Gray . . . I thought you were dead!' She was gabbling wildly, but he seemed to understand because he cradled her reassuringly against his body, ignoring her soaking clothes and bedraggled appearance.

'It was a mistake. They thought the sinking yacht was the *Good Hope* because of its size, but it wasn't. I saw the other yacht capsize and turned back to help him. That's why I'm here now. That delay meant that I'd lose the race, and the guy from the other yacht had been pretty badly knocked about when it capsized.

'Carla tried to ring you to tell you it had been a mistake, but there was no answer. Alex recognised from the TV bulletin that the yacht wasn't the *Good Hope* and that there'd been a mistake, and they knew that you'd be listening to the radio and that you wouldn't realise. She couldn't get through to you. Where have you been?' he added roughly, holding her away from him and cupping her face in his palms. 'God, I've been driven damn near out of my mind worrying about you. I didn't even know where to begin looking.'

'I went for a walk,' Stephanie told him shakily. 'I just wanted to be by myself. Oh, Gray . . . I thought I'd lost you. I thought . . .'

She was crying in earnest now and he took her back in his arms, soothing and comforting her.

'We'll have to get you out of these wet things. I'm the one who should have come home in that state, not you,' he teased her, trying to lighten the situation.

'You didn't win the race. Are you very disappointed?' The relief of finding him safe was making her slightly light-headed. She knew she ought to go upstairs and get changed into something warm and dry, but she was so desperate to be with him that she was practically inventing conversation just to stay.

'Not really. The yacht proved that it could do everything we claimed, sufficiently so to ensure that we get a fair number of orders, and there'll always be next year.'

'No way,' she told him fiercely. 'If you think I'm going to go through this again ...'

She wasn't even aware of the betraying possessiveness in her voice and face, but Gray was, and as he looked down at her he was gripped with a sudden surge of love and need.

He had been frantic when he rushed back and found her missing. The moment Carla told him they had been unable to get in touch with her he had guessed she would believe he was dead, and he had cut through the red tape of his rescue of a fellow entrant in the race and his own subsequent withdrawal from it with a despatch that had left the authorites at the small port where he had put ashore stunned and rather bewildered.

'I think you'd better get upstairs and out of those wet clothes,' he began, only to break off abruptly.

Was he remembering what had happened last time she had come in wet and cold? Stephanie wondered. She shivered in sudden need and love. Even now she had hardly believed he was real; real and safe and here with her. He started to release her and she ached to cling to him.

'Go on, go upstairs and get into something warm and dry. I'll find us something to eat.'

He was as good as his word, and the appetising smell of pasta and rich sauce that greeted her as she walked into the kitchen, dressed in a soft woolly dress that outlined her curves, made her realise how long it was since she had eaten a proper meal.

They ate off trays in the sitting-room, and this time she refused more than a single glass of wine.

Gray had switched on the television, and they were just in time to catch the news, which included an item on his rescue of the other entrant and to announce the winner of the race.

The warmth and comfort of the rich pasta coming on top of the shock she had sustained earlier in the day made Stephanie feel sleepy and relaxed. Slipping off her shoes, she curled up on the settee feeling warm and comfortable.

Her eyes started to close and, although she tried to resist the wave of tiredness washing over her, within minutes she was deeply asleep.

When she woke later the room was almost in darkness, illuminated only by the flames from the fire.

She was pillowed against something hard and warm, which she only gradually realised was Gray's shoulders.

'That must have been some walk you had today. You've been fast asleep for almost three hours.'

'I haven't been sleeping well,' she admitted, knowing that the darkness would conceal from him the reasons for her inability to sleep. She felt him move slightly, and instinctively she moved with him, not sure how she came to be in his arms, but knowing that she didn't want to leave them.

The reality of how it felt to believe that she had lost him for good swept over her, making her go rigid and shudder. As Gray felt the vibration pass through her body he asked softly, 'What is it?'

'I was just remembering how I felt ... Gray!'

He heard the agony in her voice, and she felt his quickly indrawn breath.

His hand cupped her face tilting it up towards his own. 'You'll never lose me,' he reassured her huskily. 'Never!'

And then he was kissing her, his mouth soft and gentle, only that tender pressure wasn't what she wanted; she wanted more, and her lips told him so, clinging urgently to his as her fingers dug into the solid muscles of his arms.

'Hold me, Gray. Hold me and never let me go.'

She wasn't conscious of whispering the pleading words against his mouth, only of her need to be with him, to be part of him.

She trembled as she felt the sudden upsurge of desire through his body as his kiss deepened and their mouths clung as though desperate for the taste and texture of one another.

She slid her hands under his sweater, feeling the padded muscles of his body, resenting the presence of his soft woollen shirt; burning up with a need and pain that only his love could assuage.

'Stephanie, don't do this to me. You're making it impossible for me to stop,' Gray moaned against her ear. 'I want you so much.'

When her only response was to scatter frantic kisses over every inch of his face, he cried out hoarsely, 'Stephanie, Stephanie, feel what you're doing to me,' and taking her hand he placed it against his body, shuddering tensely as her fingers touched the hard evidence of his arousal, straining at the fabric of his jeans.

The brief contact thrilled and tormented her. She wanted more, so much more, and she wanted it now, with a frantic urgency that was a legacy from her long afternoon of pain.

Her fingers found the fastening of his jeans and then the zip, overlooking the fact that this was the first time they had ever performed such an intimate exercise.

Gray made no move to stop her, plundering her mouth with achingly demanding kisses that echoed the fierce need she could feel burning in herself. His hand cupped and stroked her breast, feeling the urgent burgeoning of her flesh through the fine silk of her bra and the wool of her dress.

As her hand slipped inside his jeans and caressed the hard flatness of his belly above the edge of his briefs, Gray gasped with pleasure, and in the firelight she saw the vulnerability and need in his face, as he closed his eyes and swallowed hard past rigid throat muscles before giving himself up to the pleasure she was inducing.

'I shouldn't be letting you do this,' was his moaned comment as she dragged her nails tormentingly through the soft, fine line of hair her questing hands had revealed. But when she tugged impotently at his jeans, wanting more of him than they allowed her to enjoy, he helped her to ease them off and then tugged off his sweater and shirt with a ruthless despatch that made her mouth go dry with excitement.

'Is that enough?' he demanded hoarsely, watching her wide-eyed concentration on his body. 'Or do you want me to take off more?'

She swallowed, all too conscious that all he had on was the dark barrier of his briefs, and even they could not prevent her from being aware of the power of his body as he stood silhouetted against the fire.

'I . . .' She didn't know what to say; how to tell him how much she desired and loved him.

'Do you want to see me? To touch me?' he demanded roughly, his body shuddering tautly in response to his words. 'Come here.'

She went to him like a sleep-walker, standing completely still as he undressed her, the stillness of her outer body in direct contrast to the frenzied tumult building within it.

The firelight highlighted the rosy peaks of her breasts, and their sensitivity intensified as Gray took her in his arms with a low groan, crushing her against his body as he kissed her with fierce passion.

Just the sensation of his mouth moving against hers was enough to make her ache with need. She twisted against him, gasping with pleasure when his hands slid over her body to cup the rounded softness of her bottom and lift her against him.

'We should go upstairs.' He mouthed the words against her throat as he caressed it with his lips, but she shook her head, terrified of breaking the spell between them.

The sensation of his mouth against her skin, exploring the shape and texture of her breast made her shake with desire. It seemed a lifetime before his lips eventually possessed the aching heat of her nipple, making her arch wildly against him as she felt the onset of a wild spasm of pleasure.

'Stephanie . . . Stephanie, I want you . . . I need you.' He released her so abruptly that she staggered slightly, sinking down on her knees, clasping his thigh for support.

As he bent down to lift her up she touched her lips to his thigh in an instinctive gesture of love.

'Stephanie!' The taut thickness in his voice, the way he shuddered and then tensed told her how much he had enjoyed her tentative caress, and she repeated it, letting her lips linger and taste the unique flavour of him.

'Stephanie. No!' He groaned the protest like a man under torture, as she grew more confident and her tongue stroked tantalisingly along his inner thigh, his body tensing under its need to thrust against the torment of her mouth.

Stephanie heard the thick sound of pleasure and protest stifled in his throat and felt a heady upsurge of her own female power. She could make him weak and fill him with the same need that filled her; she could make him ache for the touch of her hands and mouth in the way she ached for him.

She felt his hands come down and grip her shoulders ready to force her away as her lips continued to drift across his skin, but when she reached higher and her nails dragged teasingly through the fine hair coating his thighs, they fastened instead in the thickness of her hair, urging her against him with hoarse words of praise and need as he gave in to his body's unashamed desire for the delicate caress of her mouth.

That she, who had never before even contemplated sharing such intimacy with anyone, should derive such pleasure from his body's response to her touch was an awesome experience, and when Gray suddenly cried out in hoarse protest, picking her up and fastening his mouth over hers, she yielded herself completely, melting against him, softly inciting him to fit his body against hers and fill her with its potent strength.

He released her only to put her down on the rug and cover her with the heat of his flesh, entering her with a harsh cry of need that melted her bones and filled her with dizzying pleasure.

They made love with a wildness that half shocked her, falling asleep in one another's arms, only to wake and make love again, more slowly this time, until their bodies exploded in fierce surges of pleasure that left them drained and at peace.

CHAPTER TEN

STEPHANIE woke up alone in her own bed, and knew from the angle of the sun shining in through the window that it was late ... very late.

She got up and dressed quickly, going downstairs, anxious to see Gray, pausing outside the kitchen door as she heard voices.

Her blood turned to ice as she recognised Carla's. To her knowledge Carla had not visited the cottage once since she herself had arrived, and she hated the thought of her being here now. Had Gray *told* her about last night? Had he begged her to leave her husband ... had he ...?

She was just about to make her presence known and push open the door when she heard Carla saying unhappily, 'Gray, I like Stephanie, and I hate deceiving her like this.'

As she stepped back from the door in shock, Gray's response was lost to her.

She reached the stairs and stumbled up them to the sanctuary of her own room, Carla's betraying words ringing in her ears. Her mouth was trembling and she tried to keep it still. Carla's words could have only one meaning. Gray had been using her ... carrying on his affair with Carla, despite what he had told her. Oh, how bitterly ironic it was that *Carla* should be the one to feel remorse, and not Gray.

How could he do this to her? How could he use her

like this? How could he have changed so much?

She curled up on her bed, frozen with shock and grief.
She heard the back door open and close and a car start
up, and knew that Carla had left; but still she didn't
move.

She heard Gray come upstairs and knock on her door.
'Stephanie, are you awake?'

If she didn't reply, he would come in and she couldn't
face him yet, she thought in panic.

'Yes . . . yes. I'm getting up now,' she called back,
hoping the closed door would distort her voice enough
for him not to recognise its betraying tremor.

'I've got to go down to the yard for half an hour.'

The yard . . . or to see Carla.

Heartsick, she called out some response which must
have satisfied him because she heard him going back
downstairs, and then within minutes the back door
opened and closed again.

She had to get away, she thought feverishly. She
couldn't stay here any longer. She couldn't endure any
more pain. She had already inflicted sufficient on
herself surely, she thought bitterly. She had known all
along that Gray didn't love her . . . but she had also
thought he had meant what he said about ending his
affair with Carla. Had she secretly hoped that he might
eventually turn to her?

Oh, what did it matter now? She *had* to get away. She
had to escape before she betrayed herself any further.
When she thought about last night, when she remembered how she had adored and worshipped him in the
most intimate way there could be . . . She closed her eyes
and swallowed.

And he had seemed to share her feelings, to . . .

Restlessly she got off the bed. Why delude herself any further? He had probably been pretending she was Carla. The pain that racked her body reinforced her decision to leave. If she stayed . . . She *couldn't* stay.

Recklessly she flung clothes into her suitcase without folding them. She had half an hour, that was all. She made it with five minutes to spare, not even turning once to look behind her as she drove out of the village heading for the motorway and London.

She had left Gray a note simply stating that she thought it best to leave. That way at least she could salvage something of her pride.

It didn't sustain her for very long. Before she was even half-way back she would have given anything for Gray to simply materialise beside her and take her back. It was degrading to love someone so intensely, especially when there was not the remotest chance of her feelings being returned.

After such thoughts, it came as something of a shock to look in her driving mirror and discover the flashing lights of the car racing up behind her.

Her ridiculous hope that Gray might actually have pursued her died the moment she recognised the woman behind the wheel of the other car.

Carla!

For one mad moment she was tempted to try to out-speed her, but one look at Carla's sporty, expensive-looking car confirmed that her own VW would have no hope of outrunning it, and so instead she pulled off the road at the first lay-by, and stopped her car, fighting against the fierce tension gripping her as she heard Carla stop behind her.

In her driving mirror she could see the other woman

running towards her VW.

'Stephanie, where are you going? When I saw Gray, he told me . . .'

'That he and I have been lovers.'

Pride made her say the words before Carla could, her chin tilting defiantly. She had no idea why Carla had followed her, nor could she totally understand the concerned note in the older woman's voice, but she was too wrought up to dwell on these anomalies now.

'Stephanie, I don't think you understand.'

Incredibly, Carla sounded sympathetic and was actually reaching out to touch her, her hand resting lightly on her arm as though she was half afraid that Stephanie might dash away.

'You're running away, aren't you? Leaving Gray? Look, come and sit in my car for a moment so that we can talk.'

Much as she wanted to refuse, Stephanie discovered that she wasn't going to be given the opportunity to do so. Taking her arm in a firm grip, Carla all but dragged her over to her car, and somehow or other Stephanie discovered that she was sitting in its passenger seat, while Carla turned to face her in the driver's seat, an earnest and very determined expression on her face.

'I know you probably think this is none of my business . . . but I can't simply stand by and let you ruin Gray's life.'

'*Me* . . . ruin *Gray's* life . . .' Stephanie began indignantly, but Carla wasn't listening.

'I couldn't believe it when I spotted you driving away from the village. When I saw Gray this morning . . .'

'You told him that you weren't prepared to go on deceiving me,' Stephanie told her grimly.

'So you *did* overhear us! I thought I heard someone. Look, Stephanie, I know that you think Gray and I are romantically involved, but you couldn't be more wrong. Please, just let me ask you one thing. Do you love Gray?'

She wanted to deny it; she fully intended to deny it, but instead of doing so she heard herself saying huskily, 'Yes, yes I do.'

'Thank God for that!'

Carla's heartfelt exclamation was the last thing she had expected to hear.

'Look, let's start at the beginning, shall we?'

'You mean the beginning of your affair with Gray?' Stephanie demanded grittily, already regretting the weakness that had lulled her into betraying her feelings.

'No,' Carla denied softly. 'I mean the beginning of his love for you.'

Shock held Stephanie right in her seat. What sort of cruel game was Carla playing?

'Gray doesn't love *me*,' she began bitterly.

But Carla cut across her objections and said firmly, 'Oh yes, he does, and I'm betraying his confidence to tell you this, Stephanie. He's loved you since you were eighteen. He told me so when he begged me for my help. You see, when he realised you thought that he and I were having an affair, he begged me to go along with your misconception. He told me how you had offered to help him to save him from my clutches.'

Carla grinned unrepentantly at Stephanie's shocked expression. 'That was when I began to think that there was hope for Gray, after all. No woman could be so self-sacrificing without caring. I have to confess, though, that it hasn't been easy playing the part you cast for me, and as I told Gray this morning, it's time he told you the truth, and how he feels about you. That was what you overheard,' Carla told her softly. 'Gray loves you, Stephanie.'

'Then why hasn't he told me so?'

'Because he's frightened of driving you away ... of losing what little he believes he has of you. This morning he told me that he couldn't stand it any longer, and that he had to tell you how he feels. When I saw you driving away from the village I couldn't believe it. I had to stop you to find out what had happened ...'

It took two hours of emotionally exhausting but steadfast talking on Carla's part before Stephanie came anywhere near believing her, but in the end not even she was proof against the other woman's obvious sincerity and concern.

Now so many of the previous anomalies in Carla's behaviour were explained.

'When I overheard the two of you this morning, I thought he had been deceiving me all the time,' she said shakily at last.

'Shouldn't you be telling Gray this and not me?' Carla asked gently. 'He won't come to you, Stephanie; he's too scared of losing you completely. When he finds out that you've gone, he'll draw the obvious conclusion—that you don't care enough about him to stay. If you want him, I'm afraid you'll have to tell him so.'

If she wanted him? She gave the other woman a shaky smile.

'And just for the record,' Carla added firmly, 'I like and admire Gray as a friend, both of us do, but *Alex* is the man I love, I hope that's understood.'

Stephanie wasn't quite sure what she understood apart from the fact that it was imperative that she get back to Gray just as quickly as possible.

As she got out of Carla's car she turned impulsively to the other woman and asked hesitantly, 'Are you sure . . .?'

'I know a man who's in love when I see one.'

'Wish me luck, then.'

'You won't need it,' Carla assured her. 'Just walk in, open your arms and tell him you love him. That's all you need to do.'

Never had twenty miles taken so long to cover. Even pressing her VW as hard as she dared it seemed to take for ever before she saw the familiar outline of the estuary and the huddle of the village rooftops.

All her old fear had gone, and in its place was a feeling of peace and homecoming. At long last she had buried all her ghosts and she was free to step into the future.

A future that would be no future at all without Gray to share it with her, she reminded herself as she drove down the village street, and parked outside the cottage.

To her intense disappointment there was no sign of Gray anywhere. He had obviously returned to the cottage since her departure, because her note was gone, and she grimaced distastefully over the bowl full of dirty washing up—that was unlike Gray, who was normally such a tidy person.

In the sitting-room she discovered a half-empty bottle of whisky and a tumbler, and then as she moved round the corner of the settee she discovered that Gray wasn't out at all; instead he was lying curled up on the settee, deeply asleep.

Gray drinking! It was practically unheard of. Compassion, guilt and love welled up inside her and she bent to touch his face lightly with her fingertips.

He made a sound in his sleep but didn't wake up. She debated about what to do for several minutes, and then decided to let him have his sleep out. To stop herself from losing her fragile courage while she waited, she set about cleaning up the kitchen, and then collected some logs and lit the fire in the sitting-room.

It was a cold day with a rough breeze coming off the sea, chilly enough to raise goose-bumps on her flesh, and certainly cool enough to merit a fire. Besides, it gave her something to do. She was mortally afraid that if Gray didn't wake up soon she would lose her courage completely and turn tail and run.

She sat back on her heels and watched him after she had lit the fire. The beginnings of a dark stubble covered his jaw; in sleep he looked vulnerable and pale. She sighed and got up to go and wash her hands, and then on impulse made some coffee. He might welcome a cup when he eventually woke up.

She couldn't let him sleep much longer. If she did . . . She sensed that Carla was right when she said that Gray would not tell her voluntarily how he felt. So many mistakes between them . . . so much wasted time.

She kneeled beside him and took his hand in her own, bending over him to feather a light kiss against his lips.

Almost immediately his eyelashes lifted. The look in his eyes when he saw her told its own story. Almost immediately he shielded them, and as she swallowed the lump that had gathered in her throat, she said huskily, 'Wake up, Sleeping Beauty.'

He frowned and struggled to sit up, clutching his

head as he did so. 'My God, have I got a hangover!'

'A well-deserved one, to judge from this,' Stephanie told him wryly, displaying the half-empty bottle.

He frowned and looked at her. 'You left . . .'

'Yes.' It had to be now, before she lost her courage completely. 'And now I'm back. Gray, before either of us says anything else, there's something I must tell you.' She was unconsciously pleating the fabric of his shirt as she avoided looking directly at him.

'I . . . I left this morning because . . . because I love you far too much to stay here with you any longer as your friend . . .'

For a moment she thought Carla had been wrong and that she had just made the most embarrassing admission of her life, and then Gray said weakly, 'Say that again. I don't think I heard it properly.'

'I love you,' she repeated huskily. 'I love you, Gray.'

She held out her arms and was almost lifted off her feet as he got up in one lithe motion and closed his own round her, kissing her with open hunger.

'If you feel like that about me, then why the hell did you leave?' he demanded thickly against her mouth. 'Have you any *idea* of what you've put me through? Of how many empty years I've waited to hear you say that to me?'

Tears burned her eyes and she shook her head.

'We can talk later. Just hold me now, Gray. I still can't believe it's true. I thought you loved Carla . . . I . . .'

'And I was too damned scared of driving you away to tell you how I felt. I told myself it was enough that I could arouse you . . . that through me you'd learned what it meant to be a woman. I told myself that if I was patient love would come, and then I thought I'd gone and ruined everything by frightening you half to death with my need for you, making you run away.'

Stephanie laughed at that, a delicious sound that smoothed the tension.

'You can frighten me like that any time you like,' she teased, squirming at his mock growl of annoyance, loving the way his body immediately hardened against hers at her provocatively enticing movement.

'When ... when did you first know how you felt about me?' Gray demanded. 'And why the hell have you waited so long to tell me?'

'I don't really know ... it just sort of grew on me ... at first I just thought my jealousy of Carla was because I resented what she was doing to you—then I realised it was more than that.'

She swallowed and offered him a small smile.

'That day when I walked into your room and saw you, I was stunned by how I felt ... I thought I must have imagined it. Paul never made me feel like that, not even in the beginning when I first thought I loved him. Then, later, I remembered you lifting me out of my father's boat one day when we first came down to the estuary. I mooned about the yard for weeks after that just longing for a glimpse of you, but you were never there. Paul was, though ...'

Both of them fell silent, and then Gray said huskily, 'I remember that afternoon; the feel of you in my arms, the knowledge that I wanted you. I kept out of your way deliberately. You were seventeen, Steph,' he told her roughly, seeing the pain in her eyes. 'The thoughts I was having about you were almost criminal. I told myself I'd have to wait until you'd grown up a little, but Paul ...

After the two of you got married, I told myself I had to forget you, but I couldn't. When Paul died I told myself I was getting a second chance, but you wouldn't let me get near you. I thought it was because you loved him so much.'

Stephanie shook her head. 'I never loved him—not really, but I couldn't bear to tell anyone the truth. It took the fear of losing you to someone else to make me face up to it.'

'If only I'd known, I would have made you jealous years ago,' Gray teased. 'I could hardly believe it when you accused me of having an affair with Carla, but I seized on it as an excuse to get closer to you, to keep you with me. If I couldn't be your lover, then pretending to be was the next best thing.'

'I've been such a fool,' Stephanie groaned. 'Can you forgive me?'

Gray pretended to consider the matter, a teasing smile curling his mouth as he said judiciously, 'I think I just might, providing . . .'

'Providing what?'

'Providing you wear that peach ballgown for me the night we get married.'

Stephanie stared at him. Tiny laughter lines creased round his eyes as he fought to control his grin.

'You liked it that much?' she asked still confused.

'Umm. Well, actually,' he confessed outrageously, drawing her closer to him, 'what I liked was what you were wearing underneath it.'

He laughed softly and dodged out of the way of her soft fists as they landed against his arm, and despite the pink flush of embarrassment mantling her skin, Stephanie couldn't help laughing a little herself.

She and Paul had never shared anything like this, and as though he was aware of how overwhelmed she was feeling by the reality of knowing that he loved her, the laughter faded from his eyes and he said roughly, 'God, Steph, I love you so much.' His fingertips traced the shape of her face. 'Right now there's nothing I want more than to take you to bed and stake my claim on you in the most intimate way there is.'

His words only echoed what she herself was feeling. She had come so close to losing him. She made a small, yielding movement and saw his eyes darken, but he shook his head and pushed her gently away.

'No . . . we're going to do this properly. We're going to ring your folks and give them the good news, then we're going out to dinner to celebrate our engagement, and then you're going to move in with Carla and Alex until we get married.'

He saw her face and groaned huskily. 'It won't be for very long—three weeks, no more. I want to court you the way I would have done if Paul hadn't beaten me to it,' he said softly. 'I want to take you out to show you off.' He shook his head and grimaced. 'Does any of this make any sense?'

'All of it,' she told him softly. 'But something tells me it's going to be a very, very long three weeks.'

She felt him smiling as he kissed her, and when eventually he released her he said teasingly, 'Not for me. Every night I'll be dreaming of you wearing that peach dress.'

She wore it to get married in, with the discreet addition of some pretty net veiling to make it less revealing.

She hadn't told Gray, and as he turned round to

watch her walking down the aisle on her father's arm she saw his eyes widen.

Her own laughed back at him as they shared their private knowledge. They were spending their honeymoon in a private villa on a small island in the Aegean where they could sail, swim and snorkel in perfect clear seas; but tonight after the ceremony, they would be going back to the cottage, and the look in Gray's eyes as they burned over her told her how much he was looking forward to the moment when they would be alone. As she was herself.

She turned to face the vicar and the service began. Her heart swelled with love and gratitude. Gray turned to look at her, the love she felt for him mirrored in his eyes.

As the vicar spoke sonorously she saw Gray mouth silently, 'I love you,' and she was filled with a sense of homecoming and peace.

Harlequin Presents

Coming Next Month

Available in October wherever paperback books are sold, or through
Harlequin Reader Service:

In the U.S.
901 Fuhrmann Blvd.
P.O. Box 1397
Buffalo, N.Y. 14240-1397

In Canada
P.O. Box 603
Fort Erie, Ontario
L2A 5X3

Temptation™

TEMPTATION WILL BE
EVEN HARDER TO RESIST...

In September, Temptation is presenting a sophisticated new face to the world. A fresh look that truly brings Harlequin's most intimate romances into focus.

What's more, all-time favorite authors Barbara Delinsky, Rita Clay Estrada, Jayne Ann Krentz and Vicki Lewis Thompson will join forces to help us celebrate. The result? A very special quartet of Temptations...

- **Four striking covers**
- **Four stellar authors**
- **Four sensual love stories**
- **Four variations on one spellbinding theme**

All in one great month! Give in to Temptation in September.

TDESIGN-1

ATTRACTIVE, SPACE SAVING BOOK RACK

Display your most prized novels on this handsome and sturdy book rack. The hand-rubbed walnut finish will blend into your library decor with quiet elegance, providing a practical organizer for your favorite hard-or soft-covered books.

Only $9.95

***Approximately
16" x 8"
when assembled***

Assembles in seconds!

To order, rush your name, address and zip code, along with a check or money order for $10.70* ($9.95 plus 75¢ postage and handling) payable to *Harlequin Reader Service*:

Harlequin Reader Service
Book Rack Offer
901 Fuhrmann Blvd.
P.O. Box 1396
Buffalo, NY 14269-1396

Offer not available in Canada.

BKR-1A

*New York and Iowa residents add appropriate sales tax.

HARLEQUIN SIGNATURE EDITION

Editorial secretary Debra Hartway travels to the Salvador family's rugged Cornish island home to work on Jack Salvador's latest book. Disturbing questions hang in the troubled air over Lovelis Island. What or who had caused the tragic death of Jack's young wife? Why did Jack stay away from the home and, more especially, the baby son he loved so well? And—why should Rodare, Jack's brother, who had proved himself a man of the highest integrity, constantly invade Debra's thoughts with such passionate, dark desires...?

Violet Winspear, who has written more than 65 romance novels translated worldwide into 18 languages, is one of Harlequin's best-loved and bestselling authors. HOUSE OF STORMS, her second title in the Harlequin Signature Edition program, is a full-length novel rich in romantic tradition and intriguingly spiced with an atmosphere of danger and mystery.

Watch for HOUSE OF STORMS—coming in October! HOFS-1